As I Was a Boy Fishing

Richard Lewis Davies was born in Penrhiwtyn in 1967.
He has won a number of awards for his writing.

By the same author

Fiction

Work, Sex and Rugby
Tree of Crows
My Piece of Happiness

Drama

My Piece of Happiness
Without Leave
Sex and Power at the Beau Rivage

Travel

Freeways

As I Was a Boy Fishing

Lewis Davies

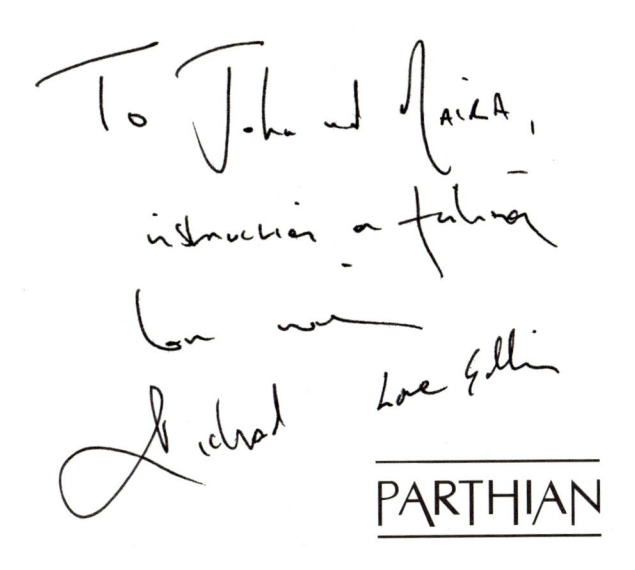

*To John and Maika,
instruction on fishing
love from
Richard   Love Ellin*

PARTHIAN

Parthian
The Old Surgery
Napier Street
Aberteifi
SA43 1ED
www.parthianbooks.co.uk

First published in 2003
©Lewis Davies
All Rights Reserved
ISBN 1-902638-32-8
Edited by Gwen Davies

The author would like to thank the Arts Council of Wales for a writers' bursary which enabled this book to be completed.

The essay *Pieces of Happiness* is an edited version of a phd thesis submitted to the University of Wales, Cardiff. The full text is available at Cardiff Unversity library.

"As I Was a Boy Fishing" & "Fear and Faith" were first printed in *New Welsh Review*. "Selling Papers" first appeared in *Planet*. "The Border", "We Come Here to Work", "The Union" and a section of "Fear and Faith" were published in *Freeways* (Parthian, 1997). "Where you from?" in *Books in Wales*. "New Views in the Old City" in *The Big Issue*.

"Spain" in *Where the Angolans are Playing Football* by kind permission of Landeg White

Typeset in Georgia by JT

Printed and bound by Dinefwr Press, Llandybïe

Parthian is an independent publisher that works with the support of the Welsh Books Council and the Arts Council of Wales.

British Library Cataloguing in Publication Data.
A cataloguing record for this book is available from the British Library.

Cover Design and photography:	Marc Jennings
Other photography:	Gillian Griffiths

For Jo Menell

With Thanks

On *Pieces of Happiness* to Norman Schwenk for time and consideration given generously.

For work on the book that it is, Gwen Davies.

Ordinary and old, today they swagger.
From red-splashed verandas, the dark girls
smile. Who does not admire them?
Which of us will passion keep so young?

Landeg White, "Spain"

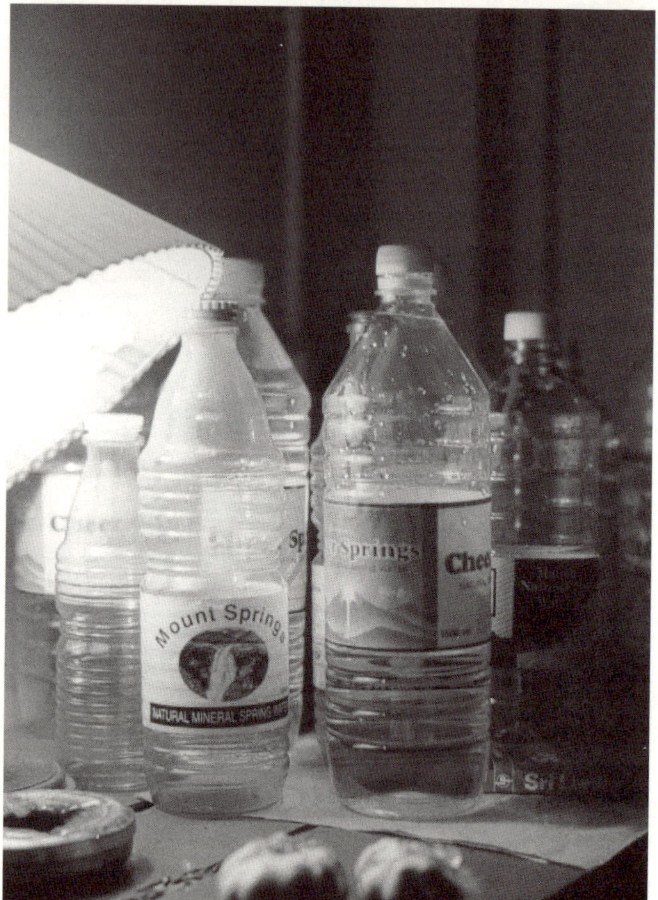
Mount Springs
NATURAL MINERAL SPRING
Springs

As I Was a Boy Fishing 1

The Border 5

The Cost of Tomatoes 7

We Come Here to Work 12

The Union 13

Fear and Faith 17

Selling Papers 27

Where you from? 39

You Alright? 43

New Views in the Old City 49

Gulp 52

Much Too Soon 61

Nuts and Bollocks 65

Pleading Guilty 73

A Slow Site I – The Cradle of the Wind 77

A Slow Site II – Still Digging 80

Me and Tim 87

Gone from Under Your Nose 93

Pieces of Happiness 99

Ella; first stop in the hills. A long afternoon hitching down to a waterfall on the road a thousand feet below. A quick swim, then a slow sweet journey back up in the cab of a lorry. Two men delivering sugar to the hill country from south of Wellawaya. Strong smells of the warm newly refined sugar.

As I Was a Boy Fishing

It is a fine day on the beach. A Sunday, late October, Cornwall. The sun is still warm this far south. I am with my family, four of us making the steep climb down the granite cliffs past the holiday homes and surfers waxing boards. We are all excited, released by the bright sunrise and clear blue sky. Pipits still cling to the gorse but the summer birds have gone. The beach rises out of the white surf, a steep slope of sand, shimmering. Although we are early we are not the first. Other families spread out on the sand using all the space they can. This is the last week before the winter sets in. A week of holiday. The last week of the season for the locals. There is change everywhere. Plans are being laid.

The first couple of hours pass quickly. We have no buckets or spades but we can chase the waves and build castles with our hands. I talk briefly to others I recognise by association. A few words. A greeting. A joke about carrying babies. We all wish we were fitter. The men seem somehow taken by surprise. Unsure how they got to this stage of their lives. A few years back Sunday mornings were for recovering from Saturday nights. The women seem younger, more confident. They had seen all this coming. A few grandparents leaven the beach. Family holidays are a possibility again.

The sun has climbed far above the cliffs by the time we take the short path across the base of the cliffs to Sennen. It is a much bigger beach, grander, with a car park and string of houses clustering into a cove to give it substance and history.

As I Was a Boy Fishing

The sea has a memory here. The beach is full of people. Not crowded but again the people spread out intent on making the most of the unaccustomed space. The adults seem surprised by the warmth of the day. This should be October, clouds and stiff winds as the winter storms wait a few weeks away. The children adapt more quickly. The beach, the sun, the waves, they take their clothes off. The experience of age suggests it is only a lull but gradually the promise is fulfilled and people stray into the water. The last six weeks of work and school are only a lull in a future of warmth and pleasure. Things will go on as before.

By two we are waiting in a cafe for pizza. It is full and the pizzas are bland but the promenade is flowing with summer now. Chairs glint in the sun, the sea is blue and old and full of the memory of Cornwall as I was a boy fishing. The cove is full of my grandmother passing out sandwiches. The bus from Penzance. My grandfather drinking St Austell bitter on a Friday night. This is the life that has surrounded me.

I take my own children through the boats to the sand. We find worn limpets and smashed crab shells. I catch a goby in a rock pool and we all touch the sticky red anenomes. They retract sharply, pulling into themselves. There are other families, playing games, eating sandwiches, chasing themselves and the pleasure of the day.

I am full from pizza.

I take my son out on the breakwater. It has a sign warning that it is dangerous at all times. No-one takes any notice. I can see the past here. A storm, waves washing over the top. Sitting in a blue Ford Escort watching the sea. Today the sea is calm and the tide floundering at low water. As we walk along the hard granite there is a shout from the beach. Gill has seen something in the water. She is not alone. People crowd to the waterfront. Excitement.

I see the fins quickly. Black and sharp, rising and falling smoothly through the water. Then a tail clear in the sunshine as the dolphins kick hard. They surround the crab pens at first. Circling, six or seven moving fast. They have the time. The water is clear and there is no rush.

The promenade is packed now. People pushing to get to the front. Straining for the best view, the most reliable evidence, identification. What are they doing out there? This is something else. Few will have seen them this close before. A new holiday experience.

A single surfer gets out close to the group. The dolphins are cautious at first, edging around him but then there is an explosion of action. They swirl around him in numbers rising clear of the water. He is surrounded. His friends edge back to the beach. Watching from a distance. The dolphins only want to see him. Soon they drift away. But others are following them now. A boat from the harbour tries to get near.

The promenade still watches. The edge of the beach is lined with people looking out. This is real, now. There is no analysis, expert analysis, guilt, bravado, we are on our own. I am perched on the end of the breakwater with my children and wife. A young girl sitting next to me wishes aloud to be a dolphin. Her mother pulls her away gently from the edge. Then the group moves further out. We are left watching flashes of black in the sunlight. Slowly we all pull back from the edge.

Two hours later we have walked back across the long open beach at Sennen. People have returned to their lives on the beach. Rock pools, cricket with children, the feeding of babies. I catch sight of the dolphins against the sun. They have moved the fish they have been chasing north along the waves to the cliffs on the far side of the bay. They surf the last waves of the day, pushing the men on boards back to the beach. The garfish which have been rushing away from them are forced into shallow water against the cliffs. There is no way out. The feeding begins. Fish and dolphins rise clear of the water. I watch from the shore. My children are tired from the walk. We have only to climb the cliff to get back to a cottage rented for the half-term week. Other matters are put before us. This big dance of death out on the water. We have no control over it but watch transfixed. The water scares us but does not surround us.

My son wants to leave. He has seen the dolphins. There is no need to watch.

I carry them in turns up the hill.

21st October 2001. A few weeks into the war.

Night carriage hesitated a day into the south.
Heat and humans packed for the journey become
uncomfortable friends.
A grasp of voices rich as the roaches hungry for scraps,
scramble. The people chatterless listen and give as a blind
man sings on a train in Kerala.

The Border

Tijuana is the border pushing in on America's imagination. Grey steel fences and a barren strip of land littered with rubbish and wrecked cars mark the agreement of signatures on paper. This is the busiest international border in the world. Thousands of tourists and commuters stray across the line every day, twenty million legally every year.

San Diego is a city powered on cheap immigrant labour. Work consists of long shifts in factories and kitchens. The wages are low but they are higher than what is available on their own side. Tijuana is a night out, tequila and excitement. Underage drinking. Clothes and cheap videos crowd the narrow streets with people. Prices are displayed in American dollars. A town on the make, feeding on the scraps from its rich neighbour.

But Tijuana is also a last stop for many on a long travail from the south. This is where the money begins to run out, leached by the higher prices even while America is frustratingly visible. Border guides charge enormous fees to smuggle people across. There is no money-back guarantee, only a night in custody and a free meal from the Border Patrol if caught.

On the Californian side the freeway south tunnels into a controlled zone. Stern metal fences crowd the highway, yellow signs warn of illegals running free on the road.

The signs picture three people in flight. They are not Americans. A man pulling a woman pulling a child. It is the artist's impression of the threat. A threat that is being poured onto the tv screens.

People running. Dark-skinned people. The music

heightens the tension. This is a siege. This is America.

Cars flow easily down the five-lane freeway that runs through the suburbs of San Diego straight to the border. The control post south is hardly manned. There is no toll. No checking of passports. Why waste money? No one is escaping into Mexico. On the Mexican side cars pile up to file slowly through the checkpoint. Children sell brightly coloured jewelry and woollen rugs to tourists idling in the traffic. Big American guards check passports or wave cars through, depending on license plates and colour. Another myth, south is escape.

But on the road that skirts Tijuana, the people in the signs on the northern side are there in reality. They stand in the bright heat of the summer, peering over the grey fence, planning a route on. They hold all their possessions in their hands. Tied ragged bundles or battered hold-alls are enough to carry everything to the North.

Once across it might be easier to merge. But the emphasis is on colour. Do you look illegal?

San Diego, 1994

A hard fast rain steals out of the forest like a knife. A bus skids on the steaming black tarmac. A baby is born at a private hospital in Galle.

The Cost of Tomatoes

It is Semana Santa. A week of parades, fireworks, and the family. The campsite is full. I had taken the last plastic chalet. Two bedrooms and a kitchen with a sun shield onto a gravel patio. I have a view of the sea, a shared swimming pool, two children playing in the dust and my wife. We are part of the European diaspora holidaying in Spain. The registration plates on the big mobile homes which are hooked up on the site record journeys south. An engineer from München, a surveyor from Leeds. All retired. All on a long holiday in vehicles that cost a former year's salary. Our immediate neighbours are Spanish; younger, with children they are enjoying the big holiday of the year. I watch the swifts surging above the watered trees. The campsite, a green enclave on the dry hillside of rosemary and esparto grass. Europe is doing well.

    I had been to this stretch of Spain before. Fifteen years ago on a university fieldcourse I had measured wave speeds on the beach. It was to have been part of my phd thesis. As a group we had drunk too much and rarely ventured out of the hotel after dark. I remembered struggling with the language and I remembered the taste of the tomatoes. The tomatoes were sweet and filled with the sun that pours into this neglected corner of the coast. We all claimed that we would return. It had taken longer than I had anticipated.

    The coast had remained. I didn't have a Spain to remember beyond the package tours of my childhood. Big white hotels and the smell of starched white sheets. The coast had also changed. Fifteen years ago the tomatoes were grown outside, ripening early for a European spring. An Easter fieldcourse was already at the end of the season. The farmers would catch one more crop before the sun became too hot and the rains failed. The coast now reflected the heat and the success of the change. Large swathes of dry hillside were covered in the plastic tunnels of the new agriculture. Under the plastic the tomatoes ripened all year, every year. Fed by aquifers, the farmers had moved profitably under cover.

A year earlier I had been in Almeria, a hundred kilometres south along the plastic coast. I had been trying to write an article on San José. A travel article I was planning on selling to a Sunday newspaper.

I'm writing on the terrace of a house in the village of Las Presillas. The house belongs to a doctor from Lyon, the one behind, a businessman from Bruges. There are only five people in the village today. It is January and the wind when it blows is cold and the sun light and fickle in the mornings. I share the terrace with the cats which outnumber the people and a flowering rose. It seems a good trade for a few weeks.

The politics kept getting in the way of the article. I was trying to hang the essay on a literary connection I had chanced upon. I had visited the church where a young bride had jilted her husband in the spring of 1928.

Maria Martinez was a bride to shine like a star on the morning of her wedding. As she walked to the church of Cortijo des Fraile she carried secrets that would leave both her lover and her husband dead before the sun fell behind the dry serrata. It was a burning day in the summer of 1927, deep in the south of Andaluçia surrounded by a Spain still ten years away from the war. Federico Lorca was a young man looking for his first story for a play. He had been living in Madrid supported by a wealthy family and a desire to write. The sensationalist reports of the murders surrounding the wedding of Maria Martinez filled a play that was to set his name shining like a star.

The church where Maria Martinez was married now lies abandoned, its walls flaking in the wind which rushes down from the high Sierra Nevada, in this neglected corner of Spain. The farms are broken and scattered.

The Spanish are not working the fields. The Spanish have moved to the cities. The farms which used to be turned by hundreds for wheat and barley are stony and open, punctuated by agave plants which rise out of the soil like stubborn giants, refusing to believe the emptiness. The people have gone from the estates, north to the cities of Barcelona and Valencia.

But the land wasn't empty. As I took pictures of the church a bus filled with people scattered the dust. It stopped on the edge of a wide field and the people stepped off. No cameras or guidebooks as they made their way across the red earth and stones, organising each other in groups before beginning to work. A long day in the fields. They lived in hostels in the villages surrounding Almeria. A growing city on the fringe of Spain, the hostels fed the farms with labour. The hostels were a short journey away from the port and a ferry to the coast of North Africa. Like migrant workers everywhere they worked for less. There was no European minimum wage in the fields. No work permits. No unions. Little control on the level of pesticides used in the enclosed plastic tunnels. Just payment in pesetas and a calm acceptance of the given conditions. The following year they would be paid in euros.

The new landlords of the plastic covered houses are growing tomatoes for the supermarkets of Hamburg, Paris, London. This is the new economy, the global economy which lurks on the edge of lecture theatres and review essays.

I knew some of this world.

I gave up on the article in Spain. I had written a longer one on the workers in California. That was six years earlier. I was still writing, people were still picking tomatoes and getting exploited. This is the way of things.

Ten days later the coast ignited into violence. Fires burned into the night as the poor Spanish fought the poor migrants. The usual results. Burned houses and cars, people frightened, people murdered, prejudices confirmed. A young Moroccan had stabbed a Spanish girl in a disco. The Moroccan was in custody but the burnings went on for three days. Headline news in Spain. The rest of Europe had its own problems.

I bought tomatoes in the supermarket on the fringe of Cartagena. One of those high European supermarkets where you can buy everything you ever wanted in the world if you had the money and the time to spend it. I was expecting the taste of fifteen years ago. But the tomatoes don't taste the same.

Six months later I am in a queue in a Spar shop on City Road, Cardiff. I reach the till with one peach. It is dutifully weighed. I am charged nine pence. I ask the price again. I am sure there must be a mistake. I hold the fruit in my hand. It is complete. There are no blemishes, no marks. I am able to pay my money for clean fruit. As I bite into it I do not know what it has cost.

Cardiff, 2000

On the danger of falling coconuts.

I like the mornings here best. Before the sun gets too high above the forest. The mornings are cool, full of birds and long breakfasts with boiled eggs. Coconuts don't fall in the mornings. They fall in the heat of the afternoon when the sap tightens to snap and they're pulled sharply to the ground narrowly missing the Welshman hanging out his washing. The mornings are safer, full of writing and short swims in the bay where the turtles dive. The mornings are shorter than the afternoons which stretch way into the hot evenings when fruit bats fly out of the forest and monkeys come down from the cliff to pick jackfruit from the garden. In the night we play cards.

We Come Here to Work

People migrate for many reasons but the greatest number will always migrate to find work.

The suggestion that the majority of illegal immigrants who enter California have come to sit on their butts while making a fortune off state benefits belies the basic misunderstanding that anyone sitting on their butts making a fortune has about welfare claimants. Sure it is possible to find the occasional Tijuana teenager who has vaulted the fence in order to have her baby in America and hence ensure the child's opportunity to have an education. Education, that common, everyday commodity, almost worthless unless it's a luxury.

The people now considered a threat are those who have travelled two thousand miles from Oaxaca, spent all their savings and are now working twelve hours a day in the huge orchards of the San Joaquin valley. They have to work and the employment a large number of immigrants have traditionally been able to secure is supporting the huge Californian agricultural industry.

It is an area in which Spanish-speaking Americans have found strength; in their numbers, in the nature of their work and their role as supportive pawns in a business that generates huge profits, provides rows of cheap food on the shelf at Wal-Mart but pays a necessarily seasonal and transient workforce as little as it can.

"These people are the poorest paid in the country. They have no contracts, they have no rights or the rights are ignored."

Magdaleno Avila is a union man. He has to be; there is no pay in the Union. Organize.

The Union

A thin, young singer in a band of thin, young musicians is attempting to instill some movement into the listless audience who edge further away from the stage.

A strange place for a gig. A cluster of date palms on a spare lot of a supermarket, Mecca, Southern California.

It has been another day in the field; no one is ready for dancing. Most of the crowd will have been working ten hours, picking grapes in a heat that would stall in the low hundreds by mid-morning. The temperature is now falling but the date palms that provide the stage an amphitheatre of sorts only offer a thin veil from the sun. People in narrow lines, west to east, following the shade trunks, make the best of things. Soon the singer will finish, ushered off by polite clapping, and the speeches will begin.

Most of the crowd under the date palms at Mecca have come to listen to what the Union might do for them. The majority are not even union members; this is also a recruiting drive. The meeting is buoyed by the recent signing of a contract with the David Freedman Company, one of the biggest growers in the area. The president is going to speak.

Mecca lies at the centre of an agricultural area in the far south east of California on the shores of the Salton Sea. Close to the Mexican border and an easy access across the desert, the land balances on the edge of aridity. Ten miles either way, the tightly-controlled fields of vines and watermelon fade quickly into stone and sage brush.

A number of speakers precede the key-speech by the newly elected leader, Arturo Rodriguez. The tone is cautious; they know they are asking a lot. Subscription is twenty dollars, which is sometimes a day's pay. Many workers are only over for the summer; when the picking ends they will slip back across the border to Mexico. The long-term benefits are hard to see: many will have listened to and believed Cesar Chavez in the Sixties, when he promised better conditions and better pay. And for a while the promises came true but now Cesar is dead and the contracts have lapsed.

They are still the lowest-paid workers in the country. The growers fail to provide adequate sanitation out in the fields; they are charged for transport, have to buy their own tools and company shops over-charge. The Union complained about pesticides in the Seventies; now there are cancer clusters in farm-worker communities.

Rodriguez begins like a man on a long road. He knows the crowd, he knows the growers. The growers have the fields and the money. The people need the work. He knows his members often find work more difficult to secure. Nobody wants to employ a union man unless he has to. Sometimes they are physically intimidated. The Union honours five martyrs. Twenty dollars is twenty dollars. But the crowd like him and he grows more confident, he mentions the Freedman contract and they cheer. He promises more contracts and more improvements but they must join. They must understand what they are fighting for; who they are fighting against.

San Diego, 1994

Hambantota; March

*crazed sea horse sea
tipping white hats at town
boat beached sands, worn dust houses
buses on the road
black goats, waiting stalls
lottery ticket losers
tourists on the hill
wind in the afternoon
of blown muslin and sand*

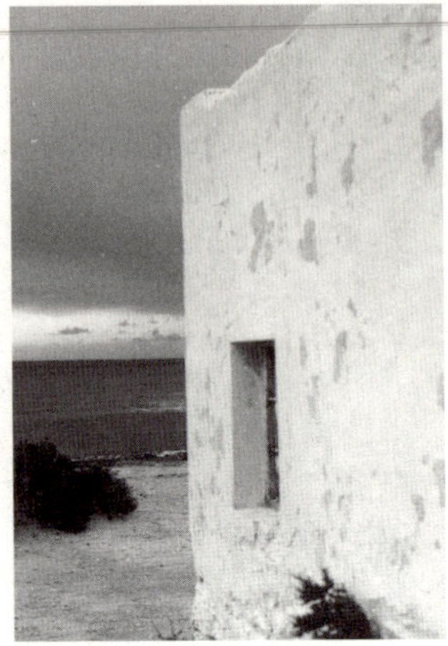

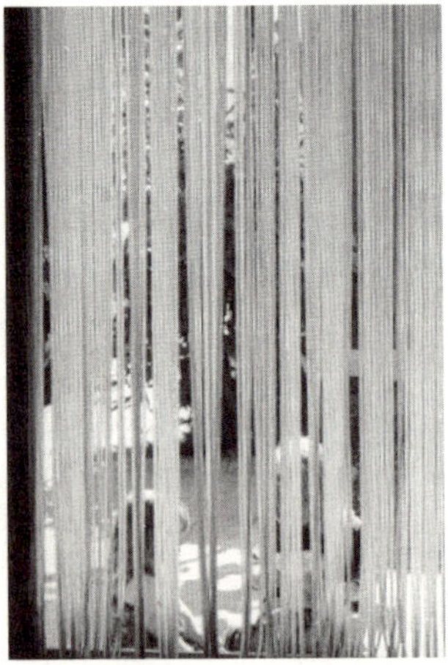

Fear and Faith

I was asked for money in Fresno. I had stopped at a gas station for another ten dollars of fuel and eighty cents of coke. It was mid-afternoon; the sun was bright and the forecourt simmered. A young man appeared at the side of the car, hand outstretched, catching me as I turned to unlock the petrol cap.

"Got any dollars," he mouthed. His eyes gazed, focusing slowly. "My car's broken down, I need some dough." The sounds slurred out of his mouth, half-formed and stained with the smell of cheap alcohol.

He didn't threaten me; just asked.

I dug in my pocket for a couple of notes. I usually give money to people who ask but I could see the news reports; a quick couple of seconds. Then a move on. Another brief tragedy lost to the airwaves.

The man smiled, black skin glistening, then edged away, three dollars richer for a question.

Coursing through the channels in a cheap motel room on the edge of Gallup there's a news item on a couple of German tourists held up in a rest area in the hills outside Los Angeles.

They had stopped to admire the view down into the hazy valley. The sun was dropping quickly way out over the Pacific. Other couples doing the same, spread out between the empty spaces.

A dodge pulls up filled with three men. Young men, intent

on robbery and used to violence.

The Germans are obviously foreign, something sets them apart. Money is demanded and refused. The men fire and take what they had asked for, then move.

The scene is viewed from the air in a channel 9 scene of incident helicopter. The thick beating of the propellers against air saturates the immediacy of live commentary. The police helicopter flashes past. Ambulances and flashing cars cordon the scene of crime a few hundred feet below. The camera scans the rest area, a body is visible, face down, shape contorted: lifeless. The woman is dead, her husband is in a critical condition. The announcement ends with a general warning for tourists to avoid unknown areas and only to stay in reputable hotels. Don't walk after dark. Followed by general comments on the effect of violence on the tourist industry.

Then the item is finished; the screen returns to a bland studio; moving on to further coverage of the election issues.

No more of the Germans. Nothing of grieving families, the expectation of travel and anticipation of return. All cut down. No flight back to Frankfurt on a Lufthansa filled with stories of football and the Grand Canyon. All lost on the fickle throw of chance. How many other routes? A change of plan, minor delays, another coffee, a day longer in Vegas added to a couple of Germans being in a rest area overlooking Los Angeles on a warm Tuesday evening in July. Any change and nothing.

Fate doesn't scare me. I don't believe in fate. Chance is too believable. Sudden death scares me.

Fate only becomes fate once it has happened. Fate is never the future only the past. Chance is the future.

Travelling throws open the doors of chance. A chance beyond the normal rhythms of living. And it is chance not danger but danger may accompany it closer.

Hitchhiking a highway south of Sydney to Melbourne I'm vaguely aware of a young Welsh girl reported missing the previous year, last seen in many of the rambling hostels which cluster around King's Cross. She had plans to travel north with a new friend to Brisbane. I can still see her face smiling out of a family photograph in the *Western Mail*, I think her name was Joanne, she'd just finished college. Appeals for news were becoming stale but her parents were still hopeful. Her father was over, talking to the police and press.

I continue south sticking my thumb at passing traffic while meeting only friendly people. A Vietnam veteran buys me a night in an hotel, an esky full of beer and he only wants to talk. A medical rep from Canberra insists I stay a night before he drives me another three hundred kilometres in the morning. His wife and child smile as they watch me eat a plateful of eggs and toast. People are friendly when you're a stranger.

Another month and they find Joanne. She's been dead ten months and lies in a shallow grave in the bush outside a quiet town a hundred miles north of Canberra. I think I remember passing it on the highway. I can certainly find it on the map.

It's another few months before someone is charged and more bodies come out of the bush. A Swiss and another couple of Germans. A few Australians. I can't remember the names but I can picture the holiday photographs in a feature item I read on the trial.

Joanne just met the wrong guy in the hostel. The others the wrong lift.

A year later and I'm sitting in the Palm Garden in Galle on the south coast of Sri Lanka. I haven't stopped moving and I'm catching up with Lawrence again. We seem to run across some of the same tracks.

The Palm Garden is peaceful, full of coconuts and monkeys while I spend my time writing and eating fish curries in a restaurant on stilts overlooking the lagoon. Life is fine and I'm avoiding the dog end of a European winter. Time to think, too much time to think.

As I prepare to fly back west a war resurfaces in the north of the island. A vicious little war that has been simmering for fifteen years between peoples of different religion and language. There's fifty years and more of quarrels in addition to the immediacy of killing.

The violence resumes with the sinking of a Navy gunboat by a suicide squad of Tamil Tigers. A week later two planes are brought down by ground to air missiles and I'm reading the news reports. Time stretches and in the long minutes my mind is convinced that the flight back to Europe is going to be bombed.

It all makes perfect sense. A sure way to destroy the second highest export earner of the Sinhalese government. Blow up an Air Lanka plane on the way back to Europe, publicity kills the tourist industry.

The head of the Liberation Tamil Tigers of Eelam is seen on the screen. A BBC screen. A big interview on the necessity of war. I start to hate him.

I begin to haul to the front of my mind a string of air accidents and bombing attacks. There is a long list for anyone who has followed the news over the last ten years: Lockerbie is first to the front but there are others. The French plane on the same night over the Sahara. The Air India Boeing over the Atlantic, possibly Kashmir separatists possibly Tamils. Didn't I read that the only thing recorded on the black box was a scream? The Pan-Am on the edge of Siberia shot down by a Russian Fighter. The Iranian airliner shot down over the Gulf from the decks of an American air craft carrier by mistake. Was there another one off the Italian coast, another missile? Then there's a string of minor crashes around the Pacific rim. Minor because the people on board were not European? Maybe just a few travellers flying into Nepal. The usual domestic American crash in bad weather.

How many more? But Lockerbie was the one that survived in detail. The fall from 38,000 feet. The cockpit lying deceivingly complete and still in a winter field. The kid's teddy bear, bodies on the ground.

It was all so easy to imagine, the brief flash into darkness, the rush of air when you must have time to realise what is happening. What has happened. Then hopefully nothing. But the mind moves quickly in the few seconds it is thrown.

The chance of that flight, return home, shopping in New York for Christmas. The people who dropped out, deferring a booking, changing plans. Why were there so many? What did they know?

All chance? What are the chances of being killed by the exploding fuselage of Boeing 747 in your own living room while waiting for Coronation Street to start on a Thursday evening in December.

The reality of it swells to fill the remainder of my last week in Sri Lanka. I'm convinced Prakarbaran is out to get me personally. I change the flight. I begin to dream, when I can get to sleep. They are not pleasant dreams. I remember another name, the Herald of Free Enterprise. I just can't picture the news report but I'm convinced it was a big one. I work in a cold sweat and begin to forget when to eat. There's malice everywhere. The days stick.

I try to meditate but I've only skimmed the books.

The kitchen wall is hard and white but the pain distracts while I'm there. It is not long to return.

Religion? A faith abandoned on the edge of knowledge and dead a long time. Fate doesn't scare me. I don't believe in fate, I believe in chance but not God. Sudden death scares me.

It doesn't scare people who believe in God, they believe in fate. It was fate, hence God that allowed all those plane crashes? I know it's an obvious argument to deny existence and there are plenty of elegant theoretical responses to show how God cannot control the destiny of each individual. That complete control would be abhorrent to free thinking Christians. So God just rolls a dice? But sometimes an obvious argument is an effective one. So where was he? Surely not everyone on the plane was destined to die. Perhaps they were, God and hence fate being omnipotent, it is pretty easy to conspire to get the required odd three hundred on the right plane at the right time and of course tip off the ones he was not quite ready for. But then not everyone on the plane is necessarily a Christian so the others are just along for the crash. Of course the true believer will insist there's only one God anyway so all the other faiths are really believing in your God all along, no matter what they claim and how deluded their present religious practices. This particular line of belief has caused some of the worst human atrocities but that's a different argument.

So this God now has all the required passengers on the plane. Being intent on a bit of drama he decides a good crash with plenty of publicity is the best way of obtaining his quota? But no? Of course the omnipotence of God can be refuted otherwise he's one sick bastard. So the plane crashes are the work of an evil influence. An evil influence that is then personified in the form of the devil's work, not man's. Or if it is demonstrably man's work as in a terrorist group, they're all under the influence of the devil. But what is God doing at this time? Sorry I forgot he's not omnipotent, in fact he isn't in much control at all. Did he set the scene and watch or did he leave early?

Of course the rational scientific argument is that since you can't actually disprove the existence of God you must accept at least the possibility of his existence and not the obvious creation of man's need to explain things, then his developing ego. Well as you can't actually disprove anything theoretically, this is one sophisticated but completely unrealistic argument. Eventually one must make a decision in the real world.

Fate or chance?

I catch a train to Colombo. I've already enquired about the possibility of a sea passage home but all the yachts have sailed west a month earlier. I spend an afternoon drinking Tiger beer in the bar of the International Hotel. Towards seven I'm on my eighth beer and the cabaret starts. The singer is good but he begins his set with I'm Leaving on a Jet Plane and a few numbers down rolls into Green, Green Grass of Home. I drink another three beers and begin tipping the waiters extravagantly.

Towards ten my ordered taxi is at the foyer and I'm soon coasting through the quiet suburbs of Colombo. I'm drunk but lucid, my fear is under control.

The war has provoked a security tightening and the car is stopped three times before we reach the Terminal building but waved quickly on when they see my white face. I guess they reason there are not too many Westerners volunteering for the Tigers' suicide squad. I'm not sure if the security reassures or heightens my concern.

The early morning flights that are timed to arrive in Europe at a reasonable hour begin soon after midnight. It's a two hour wait at the airport which is suddenly flooded with more white faces than I've seen in three months. White frightened faces as my imagination informs me, perhaps I'm not the only one who has been following the news reports. The baggage checks are thorough which allows me a trip to the bar and another boost to my confidence. I want to spend money, visa money. There's an insurance policy covering death which clears your bills.

As we wait to board the bus to the plane a kid clutches close to his parents. I want to ask him where's his teddy bear.

Fate doesn't scare me. I don't believe in fate. Sudden death scares me.

I'm sitting in a room surrounded by people. It's a big room and the people attend to business of their own. Moving around, sharing tables, comfortably air-conditioned from heat and reality. A couple look dangerous, capable of being on the edge or are already falling. Free falling down.

I begin to sweat. The amount of people. The deluge of overwhelming information. A panic attack in Bakersfield library. I must be drinking too much coffee. I need to leave.

Retreating to the car I ease into its comforting redness,

deep and soothing. Perhaps the Japanese designed it that way. After a couple of blocks I'm calm again. The car is running smooth and low to the concrete. The click of rubber over the cracks is regular and reassuring. I drive North, away from the fear, along 99 to Fresno.

Aldridge, West Midlands, 1995

An oriole calls from high in the eucalyptus. The train runs through in late afternoon, passing the church on the line to Ella and Bandula. A thick pink rose turning to dog still flowers stubbornly in the high warm air, brightening the grave of Edith and Mabel May, sisters from Inverness who loved Ceylon and stayed on.

The early morning holds beyond the window. It is February and still dark. The towns fall behind me. Neath, Port Talbot, Bridgend. The train is heading east.

Selling Papers

I

Two hours before most people in Cardiff will be receiving their mail, Pete Jackson buoys his enthusiasm with another sale, pushing the total to seven.

"It's a poor morning if we don't sell four."

The sorting office is a regular Friday morning pitch. An hour standing at the gates flogging papers before he has to make his own dash forty miles down the M4 to his day job as a computer programmer in Port Talbot.

It's still dark but the rain has drifted on, leaving a cupreous lustre to the roads polished by the street lights. A glow to the North marks the city centre charging up for the day.

"It can be nice here in the summer."

I look at him dubiously.

"Well it gets you up in the mornings."

A surge of late arrivals brush past without a hesitation of buying.

"You get very little abuse, just support. Most people will have glanced at the paper, we know it's passed around."

It's not an easy sell. Anything with Socialist in the title now comes with a political health warning. Socialist Worker appears as a double disadvantage. The concept of worker has declined, people are now employees. Working is action not abstract.

But as the main political parties converge at an amorphous centre there is more room at the fringes. People who were once happier in the wide college of the Labour Party are now finding a voice in groups to the broad left which would have once been envisaged extreme but are now merely radical. The power brokers are not the only ones moving centrefield.

"My dad's in the Labour party and even he agrees they're useless."

Ben is a student supporting an Anti-Nazi League march in Neath. It is not a town with a noticeable cultural mix. The centre on a Saturday morning three weeks before Christmas is crammed with people all colours of white. The Italians have long since merged with the Welsh and the English have always slipped easily through.

But there is a man connected to a machine in Morriston Hospital. A shopkeeper kicked into a coma in the early hours of Monday morning by three drunks on their way home from a night out. It was not the first attack. Peter Hain, a founding member of the Anti-Nazi League and the town's MP is going to speak.

A group of policemen stand guard outside Burton's window. The march has been a short walk around the ring road before re-converging at the square.

Leaflets and petitions flutter on a trestle table which is dwarfed by an ungainly Christmas tree. The loudhailers only partly work but there is a crowd and it grows as consecutive speakers take their turn to holler into the microphone.

A speaker from Swansea asserts his political party. This is a platform; despite the man dying in Morriston he must use the opportunity. The police look startled as they are openly criticised for not charging the alleged attackers with attempted murder, preferring the lesser charge of GBH.

The shoppers have begun to lose interest when three new members are introduced to the platform. Representatives of the family, they are big men, resplendent with dark beards and black turbans. The uncle of the victim speaks. He thanks the crowd for their support; there is a feeling of regret that this violence has seeped into the community.

The emotion ebbs away into the crowd as another speaker launches into a tirade against the police.

A woman with a Californian accent distracts me from the platform with a pitch of her own: "We've got to smash the capitalists now, the SWP who dominate the ANL believe in pressurising the government in power."

I'm struggling with the monograms but try to keep up.

"But the government are always lapdogs of the capitalists."

She's trying to sell me a paper. It's further left than *Socialist Worker*, full of comments on strikes and demonstrations in places as disparate as Berlin and San Francisco. She is not as vocal as Pete Jackson but just as persistent. There is a raging commitment.

II

A year later and I'm still on the fringes of the party. I've attended a few meetings with topics and questions as diverse as *Who is the Working Class?* and *The Spanish Civil War, Lessons for the Future.* The party spreads throughout South Wales with a concentration around the metropolitan centres of Swansea and Cardiff. There are branch meetings every week, a paper sale on a Saturday and an area meeting once a month. These are broadly termed public meetings with the hope of attracting a few more recruits. The emphasis is on recruitment but there must be a commitment, financial if you can afford it, temporal if you can't. The membership is diverse but most are in work, some with well paid jobs faring well out of the present system. It is a system that the Party aims to destroy. This isn't about reform. This is about revolutionary overthrow.

The Royal Hotel in December welcomes Paul Foot to a public meeting of the Cardiff Branch. *Can Socialism Work?* Foot is a prominent figure in the party and used to write a column for the *Daily Mirror*. The Captain Scott Room is packed as he talks of the efficacy of Socialism and its reasons for working. He doesn't go into details but that doesn't seem the point. This is a morale booster, if someone this articulate and well known believes in the revolution then it must be a possibility.

I'm interested in the subject of revolution. It is touched on fleetingly in the paper through editorials and the occasional column article. It is not discussed openly as the future but there appears a subtext of belief in its inevitability. This leap from reality is a wide stream but I don't find a party member who doesn't believe.

A friend sells me the paper every week. It follows the Liverpool Dockers' Strike from the start. There is no room for compromise. Collections are made at every branch meeting and at the weekend paper sales. Towards the middle of summer a strike is fermenting in the Post Office. New working practices are opposed and a ballot in favour of strike action slips through. The strike rumbles through July and August, compromises are made and rejected. Party members join the picket line.

"It's our chance to support them."

The paper offers unequivocal support. It is an us versus them approach, which turns to the workers versus the Union bosses, as a compromise is proposed. There are a lot of enemies of the class struggle. But it is a paper prepared to back people. It attempts to throw the myth that people have been bludgeoned by a generation of Tory rule to accept any management decision as sacrosanct. There is an optimism within the pages that would allow change through collective action and support. We are not powerless, we are the workers. *The Western Mail* covering the same ballot result only gives the management view with an editorial urging the workers to accept "a ground breaking deal".

By early summer there had already been talk of the National Meeting in London. Marxism 1996 is promised to be the biggest ever. Six thousand members and others converging on Bloomsbury for a week of discussion and meetings. The full weight of the party will be behind it.

III

The summer has fired a number of strikes, drivers on the underground combine with the postal workers to increase the unease of the Labour Party. The national papers speculate about a summer of discontent in a vain bid to create some news. Claire Short has made her usual blustering drive into an integrity not available for a party close to power. The ice cream vans on Brighton Beach draw closer to a point where Blair and Major are arguing over who is selling the cornettos.

London is full, light and wealthy in mid-July. The doorways on the Strand are filled with boxes and people curled away from the excesses of the street. Tourists queue for the stage and the entertainment that allows life to pass. The night begins to wrap itself around the city as the pace quickens.

I catch the South Wales coach in Cardiff. It is half full with members from further west. I tick my name off with Ian who has been given the list and the unenviable job of telling eight new age travellers that whoever promised them a free lift to Reading had been lying.

London is four hours from Cardiff, another world at the other end of the M4. We are already late for the first meeting. There are at least six meetings every hour. Spread around a variety of halls, lecture theatres and conference rooms centred around a base of London University and the School of Oriental and African Studies.

I've booked for the weekend but it is possible to stretch the meetings for a week. Accommodation is arranged for anyone who pays the attendance fee of around thirty quid dependent on concessions. A full time creche is staffed by volunteers throughout the week.

Ian is staying for the week.

"I came last year. I try to follow a course or two. When you're up for the week it's possible to be selective."

We talk politics and books on the way up. He had worked

for the NCB until eighty seven when he decided on a change in career. He's now a staff nurse at Whitchurch Hospital. He is also the UNISON Branch Secretary.

"Everyone's in the Union but it's hard to get people involved in the actual running of it."

He's been billeted in Hackney with a party member. "I hope I can find them tonight. Friday tends to be a bit hectic."

I've drawn the straw that reads the South London Industrial Mission.

The Union building rushes with people looking for others at eight. I decide on a lecture entitled *What's So Good About Shakespeare?* I expect the badminton court to be half empty. I'm lucky to find a seat at the back of a crammed hall. The pattern will continue throughout the weekend. Some of the lectures will sell out.

The speaker who thinks Shakespeare is good in parts and can be approached from a Marxist perspective finishes to enthusiastic applause and the debate is opened to the floor. There is no shortage of speakers keen to contribute expression and disagreement. People talking of Shakespeare with fervent, clear, muddled ideas spilling out in words. Revolutionary answers and the importance of being a Marxist.

The consensus finishes in favour as the meeting ends at nine. The crowds head for the bars or to the accommodation centre to sort out a housing problem.

I catch up with the rest of the South Wales contingent in the SOAS bar. I'm introduced to Dan who has also drawn the Industrial Centre on Blackfriars Road. There is much talk of a tent city somewhere in the suburbs as a last resort for the night.

Dan and I set off south to Waterloo Station and a walk to Blackfriars Road. He is studying psychology and education at Cardiff, working in McDonald's to supplement his grant. This is his second visit to London. He is not a party member.

"I'm involved in the ANL so I was sort of invited along."

The accommodation office has provided us with a map

each to find the industrial centre. Unfortunately they are both wrong and we walk two miles in the wrong direction. When we do find the centre it's hidden away in the middle of a churchyard and there's a revivalist meeting in progress complete with chanting and incense fires. The sense of the bizarre heightens as all the singers are dressed in white cloaks and voice in a language I can't understand.

The SWP has organised camp beds and a cup of tea in the community hall. I assume they didn't organise the choir which sings until four in the morning.

I head back early. My first lecture is on *The Myth of Globalization*. A lecture theatre of close to five hundred is full. It is a well argued attempt to analyse the lies of a government claiming that capital is uncontrollable. There has always been a world economy. The rise of multinational companies beyond the law is not seen as inevitable. The new colonialists can be curbed.

There is a flurry of questions at the end and protest when a man walks out after not being invited to speak from the floor. He announces his resignation to the hall on his exit.

"Twenty years I've been in."

The next contributor continues regardless. Stewards wander around with slips of paper for people to offer questions and have an opportunity of speaking. Each voice from the floor is allowed three minutes. Some breeze effortlessly through the barrier, others seem to stutter, waiting painfully for the tap on the microphone which allows them to wind up.

I attend four more meetings through the day. There's a good selection for anyone with a general interest in history or politics. An hour on *The Life of William Morris, The Genetics of Race, Is Contraception Working For Women? Mandela and the Crisis of Reform in South Africa.*

The steps around the entrance to ULU are besieged with people selling papers. *Socialist Worker* is prominent, with area branches allotted set times to maintain the assault on anyone remotely interested in buying another one. Further along the road other rival papers are being touted, *Workers Vanguard*, *Workers Hammer* from the Spartacist League, a delegation from Turkey with a news sheet and T-shirts. After every meeting I'm invited to join. The party, as any, prospers by recruitment and activism.

Saturday night and the lectures finish at nine. There are bands, a rave disco and two comedians in various sections of the complex but I prefer the conversation and argument of the bars. I lose heavily in a discussion on teachers striking to exclude a particularly disruptive child from school. The party line advocates striking for better conditions. It is the long term view. I obviously haven't attended enough branch meetings and why haven't I joined yet? Revolution? Reform of capitalism is impossible. Reality?

The bar shuts early and people disperse to the various parts of London. I can't be bothered to walk to the Industrial Centre again and spend the night in the churchyard across from Dillons Bookshop.

Sunday morning is cold and bright. The churchyard is filled with graves and hollyhocks. I read a few inscriptions to see who I had been spending the night with and then head off to find a cafe on Tottenham Court Road.

The first meeting of the morning features James Connolly. The 1916 revolution is eighty years in the past but the politics still hang over the whole weekend. There is much condemnation of the RUC's capitulation at Drumcree.

The stage hangs high before me. A red room. Red posters, flags, seat covers, red Irish woman speaking. The hall is too warm, forcing my mouth open and eyes shut.

The speaker insists there can be a revolution, a real prospect in our times. A twelve year old boy gets up and asks will there be any more heroes and follows it up with a question on the date of the last successful revolution. Two speakers from the floor get up to answer, refer to him as our young comrade but then ignore the question. The practice of ignoring the question appears to be endemic to all sides of the political spectrum.

There is a general consensus that Catholic and Protestant can be united through class struggle.

At two I'm in the biggest lecture theatre. There is a sense of excitement hovering in the hall. A debate on the General Strike of 1926. What are the lessons? Normally this is a topic that would fill one of the smaller halls at ULU or the Royal Hotel. But this one is going to fill and fill quickly. Tony Benn is going to speak.

He appears as a last touchstone of the left. Someone who actually tasted power, came close to leading the whole Labour party back down the beach. Now in national Labour politics he is isolated, but not here. This afternoon he is among friends. I imagine they are waiting for the Damascus speech. Perhaps he always believed in revolution.

He arrives early on the platform. Once relatively ageless, now ageing well. How many meetings must he have addressed. Is he here to enjoy himself? To while away the afternoon? Perhaps?

A woman takes the seat next to me. Her T-shirt orders Kick the Tory Bastards Out. This theatre has no room for compromise.

Benn speaks first and skims through the history of the Strike. Acknowledges the defeat. He compliments the hall. New Labour doesn't have meetings of this character. He then turns, his voice rising as he launches into criticism of the far left. Pessimism is not the route of political progress and personality is not part of politics. *Socialist Worker* finds it hard to word a positive article on anything bar dispute while the personalities of Labour and Conservatives receive intense vilification. There are shouts from the floor as he makes an open plea to join the Labour Party, insisting there are too many parties of the left. Fragmentation leaves the opposition in disarray. He cites

Scargill at the Durham Miners' Gala. An embittered man parading below the platform with his Independent Labour banner. Communism failed because it was not democratic. The form of a government envisaged by the party will be anything but democratic. The heckles turn to anger as he offers a charge of the reasons hiding behind the support of struggle. Is it real support or is it just recruitment? How many agendas are hiding behind the word?

A last plea for confidence in ourselves and the hall is thrown open to the floor. Again the points drift. A postal worker from Chesterfield declares he is a new member and receives a round of applause. Others make claims of betrayal by a Labour Party that no longer speaks for them. There is an anger filling the hall. The anger of the dispossessed.

For me, watching the party from the outside, the concept of the revolution seemed an unreal beacon some way into the future and the future never comes. But getting closer I begin to understand that most party members actually believed in its desirability and even possibility although conception of its form varied. I'm not sure which is the most poisonous of the beliefs. The first is rational, the second a leap from the light of reality to darkness that only a religion offers. But then how do you confront the power of wealth?

I return to the Union steps to await the bus home. There are still people selling papers. I still haven't bought one although I've been claiming to be a party member after the first three honest answers cost me half an hour of conversation each. I always come back to the same problem. Dan joined on Saturday night.

"I just seemed to agree with everything they were saying. So why not join?"

A number of members come up to congratulate him while we wait.

"We'll be seeing you at the branch meeting then."

The bus is late but we eventually slip out of London by twelve. I share a bottle of wine with Delia. The bus breaks down ten miles short of Swindon.

A month later and I'm still talking politics at The Bear, a pub on the fringes of Neath. A rash of posters across town proclaim support for a minimum wage of £4.26. The party has been pasting them through the weekend. The beliefs begin to draw me in again. They believe and are active. Labour hedge further on an actual figure. A Korean electronics manufacturer has moved to Newport because the wages are low. Principles are to be held or argued away. The election creeps closer.

Cardiff, 1996

A day in München. Big and Bavarian it spreads out from the railway station for me in a succession of bars and churches. A friendly woman in a cafe smiles and tries to speak to me. We struggle with no shared language. Then a friend arrives and the conversation is transformed for an hour. She is from Croatia and pleased I am on my way to Zagreb. It was the city she trained in as a student. Now she is ill with depression. She shows me the title of her book on the subject proudly. Her friend is a doctor who never practised and now fills jobs for students looking for day-work. He seems to be in love with this older woman, shyly but in love with her grace and charm. They leave arm in arm.

Evening again and I wait at another train station.

Where you from?

The idea of a shared culture comes early. We are different. We are the Welsh. Sitting on a Cornish harbour wall casting floats, ragworm and lead weights to the pulse of the sea. I am twelve years old, fat and sunburned catching nothing but the cry of gulls laughing into the wind. People always ask you if you have caught anything when you are fishing. It's a ritual of the holiday that the little boy at the end of the harbour who watches the float rise with the tide has never caught a fish. I answer questions quickly in correct but accented English.

"Where are you from then?" is always the follow up.

"Wales."

"I know that, what part of Wales?"

To be Welsh is to be one of the many faces of the same idea.

I share this identity with others. It is not a state of mind, it is a fact. I once claimed to have no nationality in a moment of Brains inspired rhetoric in the cellar of the Stage Door, a soon-to-be replaced Cardiff nightclub. Six months later I spent a whole morning in Adelaide City Library reading through three week old pre-match reports and finally the Sunday analysis of a famous Welsh win over England. Ieuan Evans scoring in the corner to seal an unlikely victory. To lose your nationality is a difficult and dangerous thing.

Travelling through the Western United States on money provided by a generous writing award whose main condition was that I was Welsh and could write I find myself talking to a man on a garage forecourt in Arizona. He is the first person in a month who seems to know where Wales is. He asks me can I speak the language. I am the first generation in my family who has grown up with English. My great grandfather's farm sits rotting away in a copse of bramble and hawthorn. Song thrushes nest on the windowsill. But it is his farm. I can feel the ghosts around me. Welsh are the words of my grandmother as she flits between the tongues and scolds me in both. It is the language of my best friend but it is not mine: the words have moved on. Languages are mercurial as they shift with the flux of history. To learn it now will be learning a second language for English are my words. For me it is a link that is the voice of my grandmother. I hear her speaking now but as yet do not understand the sounds.

"Don't lose your language man, you'll lose yourself. Any damn fool can speak English."

The man is Navajo and somehow he connects with me because I'm from a different culture. His language is under threat. There's a new radio station on the reservation that only broadcasts in Navajo. We talk for a while before he asks to borrow five dollars for a tank-full of gas. His motorbike lies stalled on the forecourt.

To leave Wales is to identify yourself with somewhere else. London in the late Eighties is a city full of languages and crammed with people. I'm marooned in a college in suburbia, on Saturdays I play rugby for London Welsh with only four Welshmen and suggest I'm homesick by invoking a word I do not really understand. I find empathy with people from the same background as myself. Shy Northerners who hate the city as much as I do, boys whose fathers are working in aluminium smelting plants or chasing criminals in Sunderland. We stick together sharing jokes, history and our unease at the circumstances of the city. Each time I return west to Neath, I ask people to assure me that my accent hasn't faded, been diluted by the voices in the big city. Most just laugh as if to consider such a thing would be absurd.

Where you from?

As you age ideas replace the idea of just living, accepting things as they are.

Hitchhiking along the eastern seaboard of Australia, not one driver gets my joke that I'm from the old South Wales. I might as well have said I was from the original Zealand. So it wasn't that funny but when you are hitch-hiking any words are better than silence. Writing an article on selling papers in South Wales for a Welsh Magazine the editor accepts the essay with the caveat that I leave the minor sub-editing to him. The article duly appeared with south Wales demoted to a geographical area. To me it was a state of mind and a reality, I grew up there.

Cardiff, 1998

*We land on St Agnes. Thirteen years since I was last here
with Gareth and Daymion. I can see us on the far rocks
fishing for pollack and wrasse. I write them both postcards
trying not to say anything.*

You Alright ?

The soil falls back into the deep hole. It's February, heavy and cold but the ground remains soft. The men take turns in shouldering a shovel. I can hear the wood of the coffin, hard and shiny as it collects the earth. Each man tires quickly, handing the shovel onto another. They are not used to the work. A friend of mine is dead in the grave, people he couldn't have known fill the hole. His father and grandfather watch, to me they are suddenly old men. I stay on the edge of the circle, thinking what to think. Someone offers me the shovel but I shake my head. They have an eagerness to fill the hole which I can see and hate. None of them knows how to use the shovel properly. I'm glad I'm not paying the grave-fillers by the hour.

The start was only three weeks before. Two years away now. One of those winter colds which everyone gets between November and February. Sajid had been looking rough, his walking had become laboured, the strength in his legs absorbed by the cold. His speech was slower, he faltered uneasily between Urdu and English, spluttering greetings and requests. He'd been in hospital before. Another cold, the previous winter. His mother had adjusted his tablets but his huge frightening fits had increased. The hospital staff liked him. They liked his big broad smile when his mother arrived with spiced dhal and chapatis. He was in three weeks, his cold eased and he was sent home with a new set of tablets. Once home it was just another cold as he was surrounded by the warmth of the house, four sisters and three brothers. Sajid was the oldest of eight. His mother liked having him home again. He sat in his big Social Services chair, drank tea, eat biscuits and played with his board of shapes that he clasped close to his chest.

Four days a week a car arrived from the day service. On a Saturday or Sunday he saw Simon, or Helen or Gill or me. We didn't do much, drove to Penarth for a cup of tea, walked between the benches alongside Roath Park Lake, in the summer we sometimes caught a train to Barry Island or kicked a football around the Rec. How much time do you need to become friends?

Saj always wanted to go out and always wanted to come home. The city was a place of buses, people, children and dogs. His home was always full with brothers and sisters and the occasional aunt on a long-stay holiday visa from Pakistan.

Social Services planned things for him. We just took him out. Everyone got paid for it. How much do you charge your friends?

The cold first caught up with him in November, it lingered, festering over Christmas. By the second week of January he could only just raise himself out of the chair. I suggested hospital to his mother. It had worked the last time.

She rings me on the Thursday morning. It's Llandoc this time, The Heath was full. I see him on Friday afternoon, one of a string of visitors. He's sitting up by the side of the bed in a large bright ward with a view south, over the fields to Barry. He doesn't speak much beyond saying "Hello". As I leave he clasps my hand. He says goodbye and squeezes my fingers.

His mother rings me on Monday. Sajid is very sick. He's picked up an infection over the weekend. At the hospital they've moved him from the open ward to a small room of his own. He lies on his bed, coughing between fits, eyes open but glazed. It's a coma that will last three weeks. His family stays close now. His eldest sister driving down from university in Manchester. I can see the expectation on their faces, his mother in tears. The doctors do nothing. He can't eat so they insert a tube into his stomach. The tube becomes infected, his coma hardens and he's having trouble breathing. His fits follow each other, fast, only seconds between them, they are dark retching spasms that throw his throat into deep splutters as his brain begins to hide away from the horrible pulses which consume it.

There is no panic or even urgency. His consultant, the man with the notes on his condition and the epilepsy which has consumed him, is on holiday. His case history is brought from The Heath but there is no one to interpret.

On the Monday morning before he dies I argue with two house doctors who try to ignore me. I had retreated the week before, leaving his family to the inevitable vigil. We all thought he would be dead by now. This is not his body but a corpse in waiting. The doctors are vague, uneasy, they are doing everything that is normal. I question his treatment. It ends in a shouting match which I win but they do nothing. At this stage they can't risk further surgery. It will only worsen his condition. He is a twenty five year old man who is dying from a cold and an infection he picked up in hospital. I can see it in their faces: he has a mental handicap. What do you expect us to do? It would be better for his family, wouldn't it?

On the morning of the funeral we meet in a cafe on Crwys Road. Six or seven of us. Old friends from Social Services. The mosque is a converted warehouse at the end of a scruffy street I had never noticed before. There is a respectable turn out for a big burgeoning family. Sajid's father has recently become successful with a mini-cab service. He is an employer now. Sajid's mother leads a prayer group. She is a philosopher of sorts and used to look at me sadly early on Sunday mornings when I arrived, still drunk from the night before, to get her eldest son out of bed. We have talked about God and religion. We both agree that Jesus was a man like Mohammed. Allah is another question. She thinks my body will burn in hell but likes me anyway.

She calls the women in our odd group of Christians and Atheists into a room of their own. The men are segregated into a large hall that reminds me of a gym. It is full but apart from Sajid's brothers, his father and grandfather, I only recognise the people I have come with. The Imam recites a litany. I look at the community, holding each other together in a foreign culture. People on the edge of things, the divide between Pakistan, Manchester and Cardiff. Each generation pushing itself away from the last.

Sajid had known very little of this. He was four and still living in Manchester when a strain of meningitis sent him into a coma for a month. It was a different boy who recovered and moved with his family to Cardiff. The boy who endured ten years of a school system that didn't remember he could walk or go to the toilet. When I first met him he was strapped into a wheelchair with a boxer's sparring helmet wrapped tightly around his head. "Just in case he falls out," I was told. Since he was strapped in, this seemed unlikely. The strapping was to stop him getting out. These were people who looked at Sajid and put walls around him. He was handicapped. He couldn't speak English. He was from Pakistan and his mother couldn't speak English. Only one of these excuses was accurate and that's the problem the people were paid to deal with. The rest were just excuses. I could say I don't blame the teachers and health workers who allowed him a schooling of this. I was a social worker of sorts. A fine, easy job for Cardiff Community Mental Handicap Team. Sajid was sanctioned as a person with high support needs. On leaving school at eighteen he got me and a few others three days a week. For the rest he stayed at home, talked to his mother, swore at the young twin brothers who teased him.

I got on with Sajid. He had an open friendliness that you encounter rarely. I haven't got it and I don't know many people who have. From childhood we develop defences of reserve to deflect the world and insulate ourselves against other people, they stop us from getting hurt or appearing foolish. His greetings of "You alright?" or "Hello, my friend" were full of smiles. Sajid always assumed you were his friend.

We'd shared a year of work while I finished my contract. He walked more, eat pizza regularly, hated swimming, drew round scribbles at an art class, played skittles at The Airport in Tremorfa.

Sajid had caught the end of a care in the community policy

that suited him. There was money around for people who wanted to stay at home. It was just necessary to find out where the money was. I applied to a fund based in Nottingham. They wanted to encourage Independent Living. To prevent people from moving into hostels by bolstering their means of support at home. Money was awarded on a points basis. Sajid had so many points he was off the scale. He received money to help him in the house at the weekend. He didn't want to be in the house at the weekend. He wanted to be out, so we went out.

So this was his life. It's not easy to measure someone else's life. There are hidden parts you cannot possibly know. Interests, joys, secret friendships. Did Sajid have these? I hope so. I cannot know. I remember a woman at a case meeting kissing Sajid with real affection before she left to organise more children for the respite hostel she ran. Steve was another close friend who spent a lot of time with him. They could speak to each other for hours. Steve is the man who rang me to say that Sajid was dead. Sajid's mother had rung him first.

We follow the funeral cars up to the cemetery at Ely. The women stay at the mosque. I can't get the translated words of the Imam out of my head. He praised Sajid's family, the strength they had shown in the long years since his first illness. I can see the eyes of the doctors at the hospital. Thinking that perhaps death would be the best way. I can't get this out of my head. I can't face the thought that I must ask myself. Did I agree with them? Was this the best way for my friend? To die scared and weak?

The Muslim plot is on the far side of the municipal cemetery, beyond the last line of conifers. There is a line of new graves for the winter. The eldest of the first generation are beginning to die here now. The digging starts. I speak to his father for the first time since his death. I don't have much to say. He returns some of my words. Yes, he was a fine boy. I'm surprised to see his tears beyond his glasses.

I leave before they can fill the grave.

Cardiff, 1998

The World Cup has come to town and the city is shrouded by optimism. A new coach from New Zealand has secured some unlikely victories and we've had a good draw in the group. Wales is a collective team. Wales – we – can reach the quarter finals where we will lose to Australia. But today I have tickets for a group game. Wales v Japan. We are expected to beat the Japanese. The stadium is as new as the run of victories. It has a roof but today the sky is open. The stadium is ringed by seats. The old East Terrace has gone. You cannot stand to watch rugby in the rain anymore. The game opens well for Wales, they quickly score enough tries to be clear. The Japanese are fit and keen but not heavy enough. Their New Zealanders are easier to spot than ours. I count at least ten of them between the two sides.

There are huge screens to add to the action. Most of the crowd around me watch the action via the satellite. The game runs before us but it is bigger – more real on the screen. We win easily. Virtual rugby – virtually rugby.

New Views in the Old City

It is Tuesday, seven thirty in the evening and floodlights are opening up the night on hundreds of rugby pitches across South Wales. Tonight the stories as ever are from the weekend and despite many exhortations that what happens on tour stays on tour, everyone loves a story. Last weekend we won in Dublin. Celebrations are held for a week, at least until the build up to the next game when injury worries, reality and concerns about the overdraft after five days in Ireland blunt the enthusiasm for yet another weekend away.

The Home Internationals stretch forward from the end of January, optimistic, suggestive, memory laden. Tours are planned, promises broken, weddings postponed. It is a time of movement. If only for the weekend, heroes are made in foreign cities. The prospect of the unknown, the fleeting encounter before leaving the city in the morning. There are no ties on a weekend away even if Dublin is full of Welsh people you haven't seen for three weeks. London is a trip along the M4. Scotland is colder, full of hills and dubious pubs south of the Grassmarket while Paris is a city too full to worry about the game.

International day in Cardiff is a day of collective optimism not tempered by recent bitter experience. Time and space merge around the focus of the match. Stories, for it is for ever stories that make the game what it is, are re-invented, stretched, broken beyond recognition. It is the telling of stories that make the game what it is. The day has a special candour, borne forward by a collective memory of past concerns. How many drinks have we had? How many kicks did he miss? Can we get in that pub? Don't you remember that girl from last year? It shouldn't been a try. Where are we staying tonight?

This year the streets are quiet, the excitement and colour taken away to foreign, huge unconcerned London where a sporting event is simply swallowed within the yawn of the city. A few brave Scots, ventured down to Cardiff and not Wembley for the last home international but how many of the French will travel west this weekend? Still it is a temporary thing and this year there are new views in the old city. Hills in the distance through Westgate Street where before there was only grey concrete.

Cardiff, 1998

Winter sunshine fills the city, the museum full of odd pieces of new art. Most of it culled from the rubbish. Art is business here.

Gulp – The Tour

We meet on Monday morning. The first cafe is closed so we drive deeper into Canton. Rebecca is enthusiastic and organised. I guess this is her first big show. Carolyn, the set designer, joins us at the table. We talk and I think what the hell I'm going to do. I can drive the van. We fetch the set which has been stored in a farm west of Culverhouse Cross since the end of the first run. It is rare to get the chance to re-mount a play. The afternoon is spent trying to buy a lino with Roger Williams but the price too high so Roger and I call on Gill and eat a late lunch while talking about writing. His show is about to run again while he tries to earn more of a living.

Wednesday. An early start postponed by Roger who didn't get up in time. We begin moving the set again, this time from Earthfall's green shed, across the road, up the stairs into the theatre at Chapter. The actors arrive, helping with the set on this low profit share idea. There is a trip to Dublin on it and the chance of a few more full houses at Cardiff.

I stand around a lot, not sure exactly what I'm doing or even supposed to do. I've brought a drill and a few screwdrivers and some enthusiasm, I hope.

The morning pushes on, more actors, Roland proving more than useful in set movement, top off, down to a singlet and track-suit. A subtle charm.

The afternoon is long. James adjusts lights, Rebecca edges through the blocking, teching, new words to me and finally a truncated dress rehearsal. People working for the afternoon, then building up for a performance tonight.

I cycle across the city to be home for an hour with Gill and Tai, struggle back a couple of minutes before the doors open. People waiting in quiet couples for the show.

The lights begin to go and the excitement starts. I hear Lowri's laugh as they enter from behind the audience. The voices come up on the stage. The first unsure laughs come up from the audience.

The control room above the seats is quiet as the last love scene holds the theatre tight. Then we all laugh as Roland fails to get down into the bath before the lights come up. His bare arse lighting up the show.

The words go on into the second act. Been here twelve hours now. The destructured world of the theatre. The room fills with a thin smoke as the technical support from Chapter relaxes back onto the floor. He's worked his first fifty hours this week and it's Wednesday. Tomorrow a last night at Chapter. Tired now.

Thursday. Fifteen minutes before the house starts again. Smiling faces at the door. The bar full again. I play at sitting around and talking to people, the minutes flood by and I'm still drinking.

The gossip in the bar is among actors and friends. A friend dropped from another production fills the talk. More people arrive.

Two minutes to the house opening. The house manager of shocking grey hair smiles at the doorway. Rebecca, nervous and high. Another full house.

Friday. The Dolman, Newport. A big friendly theatre in the centre of town filling with conversation and people. I sit high above in the balcony surrounded by lights, the audience arrives at my eye level and descends to the theatre below.

Again a day setting up. Newport is Keiron's home town. His father arrives on the set to see him mid-morning. Keiron is the key to this play. He plays it straight. A straight gay man and has good reviews in his first serious role since college.

The afternoon moves on.

The lights go quicker than I think and the first three dancers move between the aisles.

I'm sitting up in the balcony as the show runs but connected to the control room via head-phones. I hear the voices and Rebecca's nervousness as the first long monologue raises a few uneasy laughs. A curiously intimate experience.

I listen in now to other conversations as they gossip about everyone including me.

Orange seats each with a questionnaire asking for comments about the performance.

Half-time and the bar is full. People crowding and talking. I rush in for five minutes, meet an old friend whose name slips me but now after he has gone I remember it easily. Last spoke to him in Carmarthen, maybe five years ago. He is here with his girlfriend who is tall, dark, interesting and writing reviews for the *South Wales Argus*. She tells me the Dolman sells out for weeks with anything local but they don't usually pay a professional company.

The play performs again while I sit and write in the calm of the foyer listening to voices in the kitchen. Women talk as they wash cups after the interval. The community of the theatre pulls them in, tight to the love of the building. A big heavy man counts coins after selling ice-cream. Two young girls polish the counter, then read a script which they are to play together. The women leave quietly now, preceded by their mothers, followed by their daughters.

A sign above the counter announces "Newport Playgoers' Society, Help given behind this counter is entirely voluntary".

I still have not seen the theatre from the outside as a siren screams past and the building surrounds me in humming pipes and voices further in.

I begin to feel tired, another long day, now a three hour drive to Fishguard and the ferry to Rosslare, then Dublin. I wish I had brought my sleeping bag.

The pack-up moves swiftly and we are on the road by eleven. I share a cramped van with Becky and Lynne Hunter, an actress along for the trip. They swap long stories about past lovers on the way to Fishguard and I try not to crash the van in the mist.

We board the ferry at three. The Irish Sea promises to be calm. I find a closed upper bar and fall asleep among cushions. I do not see anyone again until we meet at the van. Rosslare is sleepy and the Irish roads empty.

Dublin. My head hurts with hunger now but I'm happy to be surrounded by the sounds of a new city. The first hostel is full but we quickly find a second. People swirl past the window.

The afternoon finds the city flowing with people. We find the theatre tucked away in the back lane. *Gulp* plays upstairs. The sink sticks in the doorway but the rest of the set manages to fall into place. *Shopping and Fucking*, a new play from London is attracting rave reviews downstairs. The management gives us comps to the matinee. It is full of pointless life, making no effort to engage anyone else. A lot of shouting and some unusual sex.

The evening finds the whole party eating pizza up from The George. We drink guiness and red wine. The cashier tries to add ten pounds to the bill on the way out.

There's only three takers for a club. Roland, Keiron and I, we barter our way into Wonderbar with the promise of comps for the management. It is empty at first but fills up quickly before Claudia Patrice, who once achieved a brief fame as the fat girl on Blind Date, performs weak voice-overs, interspersed with her own terrible charm. She is a big girl, singing karaoke, living off the fading glamour of an old tv show.

Sunday is a day at the theatre. Fixing the set as Rebecca tries to pull the show together and run three jobs as one. The Temple Bar is relaxed and full of foreigners drinking coffee in the bars.

There is much discussion and a lot of ideas on how to

break the set each night for the lunchtime show which consists of two actors on two chairs. They arrive at four and we agree to break it all.

A new hostel at the run-down end of town finds us all squashed into one room at the top of the building.

We sit through a Canadian film at Dublin's version of Chapter. The food is better, the film long and absorbing with images of winter and Canadian mountains shot through with a strange, fearsome beauty.

Monday. I walk through the city early, selling books to strangers. A city as any other. Another set up at the theatre in the afternoon. People eager and helpful.

James has been joined by Amanda, his actress girlfriend from London, they are enthusiastic and bright in a new city away together. James flew for the first time to get here and this is his first trip outside the UK. He reckons flying was the third best thing he has ever done. The first two are sex for the first time and acting.

As the first night edges closer Rebecca takes the actors through some curious warm-up exercises. I try to occupy myself with words. The theatre is half-full but the play gets a good response. I sit through it again. The space is so small we get up close, the lines are sharp and the laughs are there. After the show there is much talk of reviewers and judges. A man sitting straight at the back attracts my attention. He's dressed in a black double breasted suit with a waistcoat and peers at the show over half-moon glasses. He claps enthusiastically at the end.

We drink at the bar before heading to the fringe club which is empty.

More guiness as the cast drifts away slowly. I'm left talking with Lowri and Keith, the house manager of the theatre. He tells us stories of the Dublin scene, an actor who walked off the stage just before the interval of a Gilbert and Sullivan musical when he was playing the lead. His only comment to the audience, "Fuck this for a game of soldiers". The management tracked him to the bar across the road where they stripped him of his clothes and put his understudy on after the interval. People turn up to watch him now just to see if he'll walk off the stage.

Lowri and I head for the nightclub but at two forty-five on a Tuesday morning Dublin is dead. A man gives us a taxi ride to the hostel. I ask him questions about Dublin. He's from West Africa.

"Cities are the same everywhere, all over the world."

We argue about everything, films, plays, books. The night flashes past in the glare of a high road. Someday people are going to wake up from this dead nihilism. I hate the pointlessness of Mark Ravenhill's play which performs below us every night. Plays without life are hollow shapeless things. Lowri remarks, "I know which play I would rather be in."

Tuesday morning finds Roland's wallet missing and one hundred pounds of Lowri's money. A thief has managed to get into the dorm overnight.

Jeff offers to fund the difference with a phone-call from Cardiff and the cast from *Shopping and Fucking* collect £25 as a donation. The supportive, insecure world of the theatre.

I deliver the books I'd sold the day before then spend the afternoon running around Phoenix park in the rain, still enjoying the edge to a long run. I sleep the rest of the afternoon away before heading into Andrew's Lane. The cast arrives and the set goes up quickly. Rebecca has finally found me something creative to do. My first professional role in the theatre is shining a spot-light at the end of the first act as Lowri, dressed as Bonnie Tyler enters, singing one of her hits. Tonight I ask Lynne to shine the light as I'm planning an escape to the Abbey, I need to see something else. The show at the Abbey closed on Saturday but I try *The White-Headed Boy* on a recommendation. Amanda and I get the last two tickets on stand-by. The show is superb with four actors playing twelve parts from a 1920's play about Irish village life in the 1880's and the white-headed boy who is forced to become a doctor. The range and adaption of the characters by the actors is incredible.

I catch up with the cast at a late night sixty minute show with one woman as a receptionist at a taxi rank. The fire alarm in the next building keeps me awake.

The fringe club is as full as last night but Roland gets chatted up by one of the stars from *Shopping and Fucking*. He gets a boost to his smile and a date tomorrow.

We walk back along the Liffey reading quotes in neon from writers in the past.

Wednesday, a young woman is caught trying to get into the dorm. The police are called, she has a flimsy story which no-one believes. The police decide to let her go but the girl at the desk asks her sharp questions to which she soon begins to contradict herself. I sit watching it in the lounge, where the play unfolds. I feel sorry for her, she mentions she lives with her child. Do people steal for others? Everyone needs something. I wish she'd just left it at the £160 from the previous night but obviously it has become a habit and last time was easy.

She is arrested and taken away in a white and blue car.

I've promised Radio Wales a short documentary of the Dublin theatre festival but they didn't have a spare recorder. They have suggested I give their Irish equivalent a call to see what they can lend me. I ring them up. They are sure they can do something, lend me something. Eager to help, rules are flexible in Ireland. I catch a bus out to the RTE studios where Keiron Daly lends me a machine without even asking for a signature.

I arrive in town too late for *Vertigo*, spend the time writing postcards and thinking about Gill. Unusual to have time when I have nothing to do until six. At home now I rarely relax and do nothing. There is a freedom in doing nothing.

The get-in goes smoothly now. Then the show. I sit around reading papers and chatting to Roger, listening to the gentle gossip. Roland's date went well at a bistro in town, another tonight probably.

I watch until the interval before making an escape around town until close. Manchester United wins a football match and everyone in Dublin is interested.

Another late night at the fringe club. I drink steadily to no effect and refuse several dances. We find a seedy coffee bar on the main street and drink until four. I forget to move the van. Roland doesn't make it back. We put a huge poster of Brenda Macleese in his bed.

Thursday, a poor review in the *Irish Times* for the show. Lowri gets high praise but the play is criticised. I read it in the park. Roger hates reviews. I see him at six, "I didn't write it for critics."

Dublin, 1997

Wednesday morning. Hard to find a seat in the sun today. The children run in the big circle which is the Place d'Catalunya. Spain somewhere on the edge of this city. The children still playing in the sunshine.

Much Too Soon

It was a mixed up jumble of a day. Dorien Thomas passed me his handkerchief to wipe away my tears. The handkerchief was filled with whiskey and cigar smoke. He put his arm around me, I was conscious of the people in the pews behind. Rows and rows of church pews. All filled. I'd never been to a funeral with so many young people. People my age, people I knew. People who knew James.

Ten days ago it had been serious but fun when we'd delivered a coffin to the Arts Council. A handful of actors and writers walking along Museum Place with a New Orleans marching band from Pontypridd belting out funeral jazz. The women looked great in black. I had shouldered the coffin with five others and James, dressed in top hat and black tails had led the cortege. We walked through the doors, James read a rendition on the death of new writing in Wales. The receptionist tried to hide behind the desk as the cameras flashed while we gave interviews for the television and a reporter from the *Western Mail*. We even did a retake for HTV who turned up late. It was serious but fun. The Arts Council, through bad decisions and poor management, were killing a theatre company. We were marking the death with a funeral. James gave the final oration, death to talent.

After the parade we met at the office, drank cheap cava with lemon sponge cake and shared a family pack of roasted peanuts from the Tesco's on Cowbridge Road. It was the best wake ever. No-one to mourn but the loss of a family who were still with us. For three years the family had grown and changed with the fortunes of theatre. Good and bad days filled with light and people, a sell-out show in Cardiff, a tour to Dublin; an administrator running away with ten grand, a football game in Crickhowell. James, Jimmy, Jim, Jim-Bob. He had played since the first season at the Point, shining with enthusiasm and a huge talent. There was always a story. James had been the merry-laughing boy. A year or so out of Welsh College, a few years into a new life. He was running with a new freedom. He was dancing.

You didn't see his other sides often. The dark moments of doubt in his ability when the parts didn't come or the reviewers ignored him. The insecurity of being the youngest child of parents who died in a car crash when he was three. He was brought up by a grandmother who had to become his mother and his older brothers and sisters who looked on his strange talents and strange friends with a benevolent bemusement. He was great with people, terrible with money which slipped easily through his fingers with generosity and ease. He trusted everyone and believed completely what they said. A hard but beautiful virtue in the brutal window-dressed promises of acting. He was a fine friend.

Ten days later there is no laughter. The coffin is real and this time it holds a body. The women just look distraught in black. There are smiles but there is no fun in them. Just a terrible sadness, a disbelief that this is real. There are more people. James had many families, people who had loved him or just known him for a few weeks within the intimacy of a studio or theatre. He has drawn the biggest crowd of his career. I sit in the pew surrounded by friends and secrets. Some secrets he has taken with him. Each with their own thoughts. A priest drones on about the possibility of everlasting life with the lord. His voice nags at the awful reality, finality of death. I do not believe.

Rob and Hywel, his closest of friends, rise to give a beautiful, soaring tribute. Neither can hold back the tears as they hold each other and the fine words together. Soon the music starts again, we creep from the pews, out into the bright spring sunlight of Cardiff. The world goes on of course, nothing stops.

I keep thinking I see James, so does Vicky, and Rebecca and Rob, and Hywel. Sometimes I think it has gone on too long now. You can come back, we believe you. There's no need to keep on pretending.

Much too soon. James Westaway, a man who could make your spirits fly.

Cardiff, 2001

*We walk out onto the curve of the bay. She gets a call,
screaming into the wind.
We drink white wine and talk of books and things to be
forgotten.*

Nuts and Bollocks

The hotel stands on the heads of the valleys road looking down the valley towards the town. A room has been hired for the afternoon. A table full of cheese sandwiches, a tea urn, some crisps. The guests arrive. Most of the faces I recognise. We are all part of the project.

Peter Edwards opens with a speech. This is going to be a new departure for Welsh television. He is fired with the enthusiasm of a new job. Head of Drama for HTV, he has a budget to produce a new drama series. He wants something intrinsically Welsh. Real people, real issues, real drama. New ideas, new actors, new writers, all set in the town in the valley below. Merthyr.

The writers put forward a few vague suggestions. No-one quite knows the scope of HTV's ambition yet. We are new to television, we could do with the work. But this works both ways. HTV Drama is new to television. Peter Edwards isn't but he hasn't worked with this scale of project before. There is one voice rising above the rest. Leanne Jenkins is new to writing anything but she has some strong ideas on what she thinks should be in a new drama. She also tells us all that we don't really know Merthyr at all. She may be right.

The meeting ends. Nothing is decided. I drive back down the valley in my fifteen year old Toyota. It is June and the rain drifts between the mountains.

A week later a letter arrives with an offer. 150 quid for an outline of ideas. All rights to remain with HTV. There is a few days of discussion between the writers. Most of us are in the Union but no-one has an agent. The rights on ideas should remain with the writers. A couple of phone calls with the contracts manager at HTV produce new contracts and we all send in outlines. I write a few pages about a builder who has two daughters and employs a young man with a learning difficulty. I seem to be rewriting. I know this territory.

The summer moves on. Another meeting, again in Merthyr but this time in the centre of the town. Leanne is again the loudest. Pete Edwards outlines his plan. The story is to have a month of development at headquarters in Cardiff. Three writers are going take the story forward. Mike Jenkins, a poet from the lower middle class writing about the disaffected youth of Merthyr, Patrick Jones, a lyric playwright and Leanne. The rest of us are to wait. So we do.

The next meeting is in Cardiff. We have given up on the pretence of camping out in the town. The development is over. We have a storyline of sorts. Peter Edwards introduces some new members of the team. Claire Anthony, a script editor straight out of university, young and enthusiastic and Joanna Edwards his PA, big and frightening. The month of development has produced its first casualty. Mike Jenkins has jumped. Leanne has taken over the project, Patrick has been sidelined. We are given character summaries, plot outlines, modes of operation. There are pictures of what the characters may look like. There is still no mention of contracts. Leanne will write the first two episodes and storyline the first series. I am given episode three.

The writing is easy enough. The convention more difficult to get used to. We are given vague storylines of what the characters should be doing. I write an episode in a fortnight. The first cheques have arrived. I am promised and receive £2000. It is a lot of money for two weeks' work.

The team running the show is to be expanded. New writers are invited to submit ideas. But this becomes unwieldly.

The inexperienced producing team decides to cut back on writers. Roger Williams has decided to go to Australia and write a real play. Three others don't make the cut. Tracy Spottiswode, a playwright and animater calls the whole show Nuts and Bollocks. She doesn't get an episode. I am still on my one episode and Leanne has been asked to write the final nine of the series. She haggles for money and then pulls her storylines completely which are probably still lodged with some lawyer in Merthyr. We hear rumours of arguments and threats but nothing else and she quietly slips back to Merthyr. Later in the summer she reappears on the set when filming starts to take up her promised £75 attendance fee.

A new face arrives, Maxine Evans. She is just as loud as Leanne but comes from Neath via London. We find out we went to the same sixth form at the same time. Neither of us can remember each other.

I get a meeting with Claire to discuss the script. It needs a fair bit of re-writing. But there are compensations. She offers me another episode to write as the fall out with Leanne has left her short of scripts. Another payment is promised and arrives.

The scripts are completed and shooting begins in early summer. The whole baggage train of a film and production crew descends on Merthyr for twelve weeks. As writers at this stage we are redundant but there is a useful clause in the contract. It promises seventy five pounds for every day a writer attends the set, up to a maximum of three visits. I had spent too many hard days on the building site not to pass up the opportunity of sitting around drinking coffee and eating biscuits. Writers are not useful on a television set. They have nothing to contribute. But the directors of *Nuts and Bolts* were usually courteous to me when I arrived. Some even asked for my opinion and let me watch the monitor. This was pointless but entertaining for a few hours. It helped that I knew a few of them from the Cardiff soup of media hopefuls that is Canton but I guess some of them were just nice people. And hell there were usually thirty people on set at any one time with jobs of varying significance, another writer doing nothing didn't matter.

It was also useful for me in that watching actors work, you can assess their range for writing, the words and pace which will work best. Peter Edwards was aware of this and encouraged writers to attend but for this to really work the actors have to be involved as well. There must be consistency in the script storylining and you must have time. The theatre is a collaborative process. The speed and cost of a television soap opera allows no such luxuries. Still I remember a few sun filled mornings in Merthyr watching people work. I never stayed for the afternoons.

Towards the end of the summer the shooting has been completed. The video is being edited and the results scanned. The writers are invited to the office at HTV to assess the result. It is suggested we take two days viewing the episodes and another two to discuss the result and contribute to a way forward. Although the series has yet to be screened, Peter Edwards is committed to a second series. There is a clause in the HTV contract that stipulates that the channel must produce fifteen hours of original drama per year. The only way to economically produce this is through a mass produced serial. Individual dramas would exceed the budget.

This is all good news to me. It suggests more commissions and more money. I have already managed to buy a decent second hand car on the proceeds of the first.

Watching the series for the first time was interesting for the first couple of episodes. Those written by Leanne are still the most successful of the show. They introduce with pace a range of new characters in a number of family and group settings based around a stag night and a wedding. My episode, number three, is low-key but effective enough without ever being exciting. Three years on I can remember very little about it except for an argument betweeen the new in-laws.

I can remember more about the meeting but wish I didn't.

I don't think soap is designed to be watched in blocks and by the second day my head is reeling from the inanity of it all. The stories work when drip fed to an audience but more than one in twenty four hours produces an overdose. There should be a health warning. But then I am not used to watching much television.

Arguments rage between a couple of the writers over the changing of certain aspects of their script when finally translated to the screen. There are changes to my script but I'm happy enough to enjoy the director's interpretation. Neil Docking is particularly keen on the sanctity of the written script. He is another writer brought into the show after the Leanne debacle. He really wants to be a director and has already made some short films. He is also a bit of a stand up comedian and enlivens the day with funny stories, many of which turn out to be about his sex life. His partner in this and his sex life is Maxine who struggles to keep up with his rapid parodies with a salacious humour of her own.

The week ends with a few casualties: David Harris just walks out of the door on Thursday afternoon and never returns. I lurch between fighting over the whole process and reminding myself it is only television.

We had been asked to consider the whole week as development for which we wouldn't get paid. All the writers agreed in principle but moaned about it in practice. Delyth Evans, a writer experienced in Welsh language television, considered this imposition exploitation. Peter Edwards, on a foray into the viewing room was asked straight by Delyth was he going to pay the writers an attendance fee because she felt the work was valuable and it was costing her money in babysitters. Peter agreed to a daily fee of £80. I had just made £400 on Delyth's guts. I thought about buying her a bouquet of flowers but she is married to the head of contracts.

The show is officially launched in late September with a screening at the Plaza in Merthyr. It is a cinema with pretensions to being a bingo hall. Paint flakes from the wall and green neon signs warn of emergency exits. There is a long queue to get tickets but once inside, the cinema is half empty. The first two episodes are shown and there is a speech by the mayor of the town wishing HTV a long and successful series. He jokes that they will be running coach trips to see the locations next summer. The full *Nuts and Bolts* experience.

The series is screened in October. It gets an early evening slot at 6.30pm. It receives decent reviews and more importantly for HTV and us, good viewing figures. I continue to write for it for another two series. More script meetings, fewer arguments, more money. A living out of writing based on twenty four minutes of video per episode. It paid for a couple of holidays in Spain.

Peter stuck to his ideas of development. The second series found a few writers directing episodes and a number of actors had found agents. The costs went up. Some of the acting became considerably better. The storylines got worse. The writing seemed about the same. HTV experimented with transmission times and new publicity stunts. When an extra died in a car crash on the mountain road half the cast turned up for the funeral. There was even a picture in the *Western Mail*.

This winter they changed the writing team. I had been prewarned by David. I knew what was coming. Claire rang to say she wanted to have a chat about future developments. We meet in a cafe on Wellfield Road. She talks about how the series has changed. It is not a drama anymore but a soap. I thought it was always a soap. The ambition has changed. She talks about the pressures she is under to storyline twenty four episodes with eight different writers. She talks about possibilities of other projects. Neil Docking is to write twenty episodes. A few new writers are to be drafted in. I didn't make the cut.

Cardiff, 2001

Sunlight in a summer park. Sunday, Palma. The children are playing on a trampoline. The park falls away to the harbour. I listen to the cries of children, mine and others.

It is early in the season. The beach is cold in the morning. We make a scale model of Barcelona complete with Parc Guel, Familiae Sagrada, pigeon square and the aquarium.

Pleading Guilty

It is May and summer is just beginning to touch the city. The white, newly washed buildings which guard the park play with the sunshine and the flowers which are lined to attention, secure in weeded beds. It is a city to be alive in, despite the crowds and the traffic. People move, heading to work, the journey through the day. I have an appointment of sorts with a friend.

The case is listed for eleven on the neatly typed register that has been pinned to the board. It is a list of possibilities, people versus the crown. My friend's name is half-way down. I haven't seen Peter for a few weeks. He had called around and asked me to write him a character reference. He was criticising his lawyer for not being efficient enough with the case. There were procedural problems I didn't understand and an adjournment she had refused to apply for.

The case was fixed into May. He has been on bail for nine months. Everyone including the police thinks he has been lucky to get bail.

The atrium of the courts seems calm, set apart from the acts of justice or retribution playing beyond the walls of the corridors. The centre is the booking hall. The court boards listing the daily entertainments with titles and viewing times. I recognise an actor I had last seen in an awful version of John Godber's *Up and Under* at the Sherman. He has put on weight and looks miserable, dressed in the black robes of a barrister. Obviously acting hadn't worked out.

I talk briefly to Peter, vying for time with his solicitor and

Pleading Guilty

his wife. I'm not sure what you can say. It is beyond all of us now. This long process has surged with a terrible momentum of its own and we're all now waiting.

I make my apologies. The morning is already running late. The show has been delayed. I decide to catch the end of the case now running in court number seven.

It is only half full. I am in time to hear the final plea. This is a sentencing hearing only. The three kids from Ely have already pleaded guilty to a charge I deduce from the mitigation is robbery with menace. The menace in this case being a knife pulled on a one time friend.

Each of the three has their own counsel. This is a legal aid case. Each counsel makes the case for mitigation long and laboriously. They are terrible actors and their boredom stifles any urgency or even belief in their words. They know the kids are guilty, they have read the evidence, the depositions of witnesses and liars. They have been well paid for this but the money will not cover their own lies.

The pleas are based on the hope that the boys will be good boys now. The experience of remand has frightened them. One has even been offered a job by an uncle in a garage. Surely this judge will not deny them a chance, another go? They are only seventeen.

But then there is the crime. A crime that has to be paid for. These boys have robbed a girl at knife point. They have threatened a life for a car and thirty quid in cash. It is clear that the victims stand high in the judge's mind as he begins to summarize the case. Everyone knows that the boys are guilty. Is he going to allow them to get away with three months in a remand centre and some community service? The families lean closer in the gallery as his words fill the cramped dark courtroom.

He is a small insignificant man with white loose skin but he straightens as he finishes the sentencing. For two of the boys the remand centre is going to be the end of their time controlled by the state. But the third, the leader in the eyes of the judge, the one who held the knife is not going home to a job at his uncle's garage. He is going down for two years.

The galleries erupt in protest. The boy stands up in the dock and shouts at the judge, "You can't do that." But he can and the shouts quickly subside with a threat from the bench. There are others who could be held in contempt. The families move away. The court empties and I wait for the next performance.

Peter, despite a line of deputations from community leaders, policemen, friends and a judge who had to stand down from his case because of personal interest, will be sentenced. There are mitigating circumstances. He had phoned the police to inform them of his crime and had made sure everyone was out of the building before he tried to set it alight. Not much of it burned, he only managed to singe a few curtains. His crime of violence is against property but that will not be treated lightly.

He gets two years but will be out the following summer. His wife cries as the barrister suggests an appeal is hopeless. It is already the lightest possible sentence and the crime is not in dispute.

He writes me a string of letters from a low security prison in the West Country. He does well at first, he is on library duty and can read as much as he likes, difficult French books on philosophy and life that were the subject of his doctorate, but eventually the system, as it always will, gets to him and he suffers badly the last few months.

We still meet for breakfast on Salisbury Road. He is writing a book. The subject changes but he is always writing a book. He has never let me read any of it.

Cardiff, 2001

I'm half-drunk from four glasses of white wine with sardinas for lunch. She's colouring in a magic dragon I drew this morning. The sky, she tells me, is the same colour as the sea in Spain. Palm trees in the garden, sparrows calling in the leaves. The sun has gone behind the ridge to the west. I've opened a bottle of rosé, which is rough in that don't care for the world Spanish way.

An hour or so before the light goes. A dark, cloud-filled, rain-washed day in February. I'm in a room high above the Rambla. The noise of the city twists away below me. My two children asleep on the double bed, snore into the evening. I'm happy enough in the half-silence of snores and traffic from below.

A Slow Site I
The Cradle of the Wind

8.10am, Sunday, 19th May. Mark is already on site. It's a flat plot of grass on a hill in the village. Crud-yr-Awel. Growing up in the village my father had warned me if I went into the building trade he would cut my hands off. But he had always promised we would build a house together. It is early summer and the promise is waiting. The JCB waits for orders. Sunday is wet and quiet. The rain falls silently, straight.

The plot is blocked by a pair of pallets nailed into a brick wall which fronts onto Crud-yr-Awel. There's just enough room to drive the machine in and later the lorry.

My father laughs as I insist on a photograph but rushes to the van for a pick and shovel. We stand on the uncut grass, smiling into the camera and a flash for the rain.

Mark decides to skim the turf first. We will dig the trenches later. The machine moves with a strange elegance as it paces the plot. Cornering, then cutting. The controls move easily between Mark's fingers. I remember I used to play rugby with him six or seven years ago. He scored a try in a cup final we played on the Gnoll against Banwen. We were winning at half-time before Banwen changed tactics and decided to beat us up instead. It was a long second half. He got married the season after that and took a job on the machines. I haven't seen him much since.

We move a few blocks and old bricks for something to do. The machine out-paces anything we can manage usefully.

My father decides he can't do anything for an hour here but there may be work lurking around on the other site he is developing in Skewen. I am left alone watching the machine and a single blackbird which is attracted by the cut soil. It is obviously feeding chicks and picks up a stomach full of worms and white maggots which have been thrown out of the turf. It seems to prefer the maggots. The chicks must be young as it is only the male bird that appears. The brown female must be sitting on the chicks keeping them out of the cold rain. The bird is cautious at first but gains confidence and works right up to the wheels of the machine.

One of my new neighbours above waves from his garden. I cross the plot to shake his hand and introduce myself. He seems friendly enough. His kids had been watching the work since we started, looking out from the high bay window which overlooks the site of the new house. I guess it's going to spoil their view but he doesn't seem too concerned about it. My new neighbour is from Bristol but teaches physics in Swansea. His wife went to the same school as I did. She must be my age or just a shade younger. We knew the same headmaster. I can't think who went to Bristol University but we shall see.

I invite him to join the rugby club. He claims he used to play full-back at school and looks like he could do with some Saturday afternoons out. He doesn't seem too keen on training but offers us water for our site. We'll need a long hose-pipe.

The lorry arrives and Mark fills it quickly. Three skip loads in fifteen minutes. It would have taken us three days with a pick and shovel.

They're tipping the earth at the rugby club so the lorry returns quickly each time. The driver is from Rhos. I don't know him but he has a young boy out with him who I assume is his son. I speak to him between loads. Sunday morning working.

He needs the extra cash. His family is growing. The boys listens but won't speak to anyone. His new father explains the family.

"He's not mine but hers, but we've just had one."

I guess they're both his now.

My father arrives back, then Gareth for the first time to see how his machine is progressing. I can remember my father renovating a farmhouse for him outside Rhos a few years back. It was my first full week of work. Gareth and his machines have been a occasional fixture on my father's sites since Gareth first started his business twenty years ago. My father was coaching Bryncoch, Gareth was playing for Bryncoch on his way to Neath and first class rugby. We used to watch him play. He was big, fast and frightening. Gareth now coaches Bryncoch. I'm playing for Bryncoch. We don't talk about rugby.

We discuss the site, it's going to be a big bungalow. There's drains we need to tie in at the back. The digging has turned over a large amount of ash just beneath the surface of the turf. My father remembers it used to be a tennis court. He used to pass it on his way to school fifty years ago. This is good news. It drains easily.

We mark out the footings for the machine. The plans, fine on paper, are too big for the reality. I hadn't checked them before I bought the land. My father arbitrarily lops a metre off the width of the lounge.

The blackbird is still working hard as we break for lunch.

We're late and my mother complains. But we're always late for lunch on the weekend. My father has been late for thirty years on the weekend.

We eat quickly. Talking about the bungalow and prospects for a sale. My mother appears pleased to have me home. I haven't been back for a few weeks.

Mark is already digging again by the time we get back. My father rushes to see it's in the correct line. Decides it's not then changes his mind again.

We decide to move the manhole and have to dig around it

in the mud. Six heavy lintels and a pile of bricks come out of the ground in an hour. They'd been down there for fifty years. I can still read the name of a long demolished brickworks in Llanelli on the stone.

Jonathan arrives for a chat in the afternoon. He's big and enthusiastic. I've been planning the house for six months. He'd arranged the mortgage for me and has sold me an endowment policy courtesy of the Pearl. Today he's dressed for the training field, baggy shorts and muscles. He plays centre but we've been trying to convert him to prop. We talk about buying a boat for fishing later in the Summer. It's a dream we've kicked around for a few years while fishing off the rocks on the Gower.

An hour later Tim arrives, Jonathan's partner in crime at the Pearl and our prospective third party in the boat idea. He's thinking of building a house and asks me about mortgages.

Towards three Mark finishes. We clean up the trench and wash the road where the lorry has left muddy tyre tracks. It's been a good first day despite the rain.

As we leave a woman across the road offers us tea.

A Slow Site II
Still Digging

20th of May. I'm held up in Cardiff writing. Dad and Yuan spend the day re-digging one of the trenches that wasn't cut straight. It rains heavily and they are there until six. A good day to miss.

21st. I drive down to see it. Water fills the trenches. We decide to wait until June to concrete.

Early June. A day clearing the site. My father on holiday. Four van loads of earth to the club. The woman across the road makes me tea.

June drips through in a rush of rain and low cloud. My father abandons the site in favour of another offer in Crynant. By late July I manage to persuade him to start again.

26th. The dry weather has taken a long time. I arrive early from Cardiff with Simon. Simon has a car, a surfboard and some enthusiasm for digging. Yuan and my father already on site. Yuan is from the village. He's on sabbatical from something. We're not sure what and neither is Yuan. We had talked about teaching English in Vietnam on the last site.

They show us the shovels, just in case we can't recognise one, then the general direction to dig and leave us to it.

Work until ten-thirty digging mud that has fallen into the trenches. The neighbour appears and I reintroduce myself. His name is Sed. I'd forgotten but remember it was something unusual.

Dad returns from Crynant. We need to keep digging, to go deeper. I had thought we had finished. Stop for lunch in my parents' house. This is luxury, usually it's upturned crates, breeze blocks and tea out of thermos flasks. Simon seems to have been enjoying himself working hard.

We have to return early, the building inspector is due. Sed is renovating his windows. A teacher on the first week of his holidays looking for something to do. The inspector arrives, looks around quickly, not much to see and he's not keen on getting down into the bottom of the trench where I am six foot down and still digging. The base course of bricks to an old cesspit is still another two feet away.

By late afternoon I'm covered in muck and have been forced to bucket water and clay out of the hole. It keeps going.

Dad returns once more from Crynant at five. Perhaps we shouldn't have gone so deep.

Another week. Dad, Simon and I mix concrete for the footings. A long day.

Another day. More concreting then begin blocking. Yuan arrives after lunch with a digital camera on loan from some production company interested in making real-life documentaries. Yuan has another life as a film-maker. I talk about writing, Simon about philosophy and my father about being an employment agency for useless graduates.

Friday. We continue blocking up. Simon hasn't come West today. Jonathan arrives in late afternoon with a big trout he has caught on a reservoir above Pont-rhyd-y-fen. We arrange to play squash after I've finished.

Monday. Early morning from Cardiff. I dodge the fare on the train, my father is waiting on the taxi rank with his big orange van menacingly taking up two spaces. We start levelling the site, filling in the corners with earth from the trenches. It goes slowly. I need to make a few calls at breakfast which disturbs the rhythm but I sell a few books.

The day warms up and I spend the afternoon mixing concrete for filling between the breeze blocks.

Tuesday. Tired after a night winning the quiz competition with Yuan at The Bear. The first prize was four pints of lager. We were drunk by the time we won. We continue clearing and levelling the interior. More ash appears from the old tennis court. Spend the day doing just this with the help of a petrol iron. A big heavy machine which struggles to move forward so I have to drag it backwards. Then I discover it has a gear system.

On my own in the afternoon, I slow down, taking things easy, talk to Sed, enjoy the sunshine. Then my father returns and life picks up again.

Five tonnes of hardcore arrives by lorry at four. We barrow it in. I re-design the interior and my father reluctantly agrees. I ring the architect who is supposed to be supervising the job, he agrees to attend tomorrow but otherwise is not pleased by our cavalier approach to restrictions and regulations.

Wednesday. Simon and I drive down early from Cardiff. For the first hour we shovel more filling into the site, limestone pebbles, half the size of a fist. We take half a day to fill it. The smaller ash for the top arrives as we leave. Eleven tonnes of it. The driver takes the gate with him on the way out.

Thursday. Simon and I begin to concrete. I take an hour off to pick up a DAT recorder from Gurt Thomas at the BBC in Swansea. I've sold them an idea about hitch-hiking as a radio documentary. I'm not sure what DAT stands for. I offer Gurt a job for the afternoon but he doesn't seem too keen. The BBC is suffocating him but I don't think he wants a career on site. We mix concrete most of the afternoon but never get as far as we like. Finish at five as I watch the clock.

The site at Crynant takes over.

A Year Later

Restart after a year. Pleased to get going again. I'm first on site with my father. Des works on the bricks. He's a long retired bricky but my father has invited him back for a few days to get him out of the house for a change. Simon is still job-sharing a few weeks to pay off his overdraft. The first couple of days enlivened with the birth of my son, Tai. Not on site but in a rush of blood and mucus at The Heath hospital in Cardiff. He is at home with his mother oblivious to the career on site which awaits him.

The site starts up again and we have visitors. The architect complaining, the building inspector complaining. Then the planning authority reacting to a complaint. My father carries on.

The first month goes quickly and we are soon putting the roof up. The first on a blaze of early summer sunshine and optimism.

Tuesday. Late May. Bright cold day. Sun and snow showers as Yuan, my father and I grapple with the roof in the wind. Head clear today, the alcohol of Friday morning brushed away by the breeze. Yuan and myself enjoying it, kidding we could do this for a living despite our bleak summer in Crynant last year. I worked one week without speaking and Yuan asked to be taken home one Thursday because he'd had enough. We both drank too much cheap red wine. But this is this year and my father ploughs on. The house will go up eventually. Dinner at home, the only caller all day to the site, Ronnie Watkins to borrow a van.

Thursday. Back for two days. Filling in. Greeted by a blocked drain. Spend most of the morning trying to push it out with an improvised rod of bamboo and hose-pipe. The others continue with the roof. Finally clear it after lunch. Cut my hand on a cracked pipe. Afternoon more digging and a quick run back to Cardiff. I spend the evening in the Infirmary getting four stitches in my finger.

Friday. Simon picks me up from the house. By the time we arrive on site my father is already on the roof. A day of finishing off the chimney for my father, more digging for Simon and I. My father moans at me, I just want to watch and talk with him today but he's in too much of a rush for that. Won't listen to my suggestions for future plots, too many commitments. My schemes never work he says as he finishes a fine chimney on one of them.

Simon and I talk about Australia. On the way back we pick

his surfboard up from Porthcawl then talk more about politics and Australia. I like to hear him speak of the odd jobs he's had, knowing I won't do that now. The evening rain sets me thinking and I ponder America in the winter, staying with Madeline and Paul.

Wednesday. Late May. Warm day hammering slates into the roof. My father moans about straight uneven lines, reckons Simon's doing it better than me. I make a few phonecalls and postpone Thursday. Keith Griffiths complains about the use of his electricity just days after he offered us anything we wanted out of his garage. He wanted a free UPVC window. I think the sun had got to him. Other men appear on site, Barry the electrician, two boys fitting windows and doors from Skewen. Simon Reynolds, a plasterer from Skewen who has married my cousin. The house moves on.

Friday the 29th. Back for a final day before Dad takes two weeks in Majorca. The bonnet on Simon's rusting VW blew open on the motorway the day before and we drive warily down. The firm value of the house impresses today, the solidity of the walls. Barry works all day, a quiet sociable man. Life comes down from the attic in the shape of wires curling down to proposed sockets. I spend the day in the shade finishing off doorways and putting up a lintel across the dining room.

Good easy day.

Neath, 2001

The children are building castles in the rain and the wind on the beach at Alcudia. I remember this place from twenty years ago with my parents. I caught a mullet from the jetty. The jetty is still here.

Me and Tim

Tim is on the telephone. He wants me to attend a business breakfast club in Neath. It is a fifty minute drive down the motorway on a Friday morning to Neath. This will be the third meeting in the year that he has organised. I've given my excuses for the first two but I'm curious. It is being held in the Cimla Court Hotel, an establishment of dubious charm with Gothic towers that look out over the town. It specialises in wedding banquets but is keen on diversifying. I'm a few minutes late for the 8.30 start. I meet Jonathan in the car park. There's a group of men in the bar, shuffling uneasily, drinking orange juice. They are all over fifty. I don't recognise anyone apart from Raymond Michael, Tim's father and Clive, Tim's business partner.

We are ushered into the breakfast room. There is a low uncertain conversation among the breakfast men. I sit opposite Jonathan as the food is swiftly served. A few of the men pick uneasily at the food before stopping, realising. Once the food has been served, Tim stands, welcomes everyone and asks the minister of his new church to say grace.

I dip my head, listening to the words.

I had gone to see Tim's mother in August. She had seemed well to me. The same Marlene who had been part of us growing up in Neath. She had always cooked us chips for tea. She had always been effusive, enthusiastic for life, the love of her boys and warm and welcoming to any friends that Tim brought home. My grandmother lived across the road. Tim's father had sub-contracted as a carpenter on some of my father's sites. I had shared an egg collection with Tim's older brother, Gary.

We talk of the old times while I drink two cups of tea and eat the digestives Raymond has brought in from the kitchen. She knows she has only a few months to live. The cancer is growing quickly and the doctors have suggested there is no cure. The phone rings constantly in the hour I am at her house. Friends catching up, talking to her. The same house of Tim's childhood.

No-one seems to move in Neath, once the children are born. Children who moved away with their parents seem to be still children to me. Jonathan Tweed, Adrian Belchum, Stuart Fellows. Still twelve year old boys. For Tim and me things are more complicated. We have shared a lot: fishing late in the evening on the Dyffryn. I can see my worm hitting the water below the rapids and catching two trout in a row while Tim caught nothing. He always wanted to know if we were going to catch something. His enthusiasm for fishing infectious.

Girls, drinking, rugby: all shared passions, sometimes sharing. A girlfriend of his once hit me across the face in the Talk of the Abbey nightclub. I lived in squalor and laughter in a house with him and six others at university. Good times. Tim was one of the best rugby players, five or six mercurial seasons for Swansea when he might have had a handful of Welsh caps. He could break a game for you, conjure a try from forty yards out of nothing but deception and pace. He could run faster backwards than I could forwards. And we've finished with all that now.

After breakfast the speaker is introduced. Graham Davies, another friend of Tim. He was a sharp small winger for Neath when we were all just begining with senior rugby. Tim was soon to go to Swansea. I remember watching Graham against a few of the big sides, Bath, Cardiff. He won a couple of B caps without getting into the full Welsh team.

He is here to talk about his religion. He has always been a Christian. How it has affected his career, helped him with success in sport and now in business. He met his wife in a Christian meeting at college. He tells a few stories, almost apologetically, not sure of his audience, perhaps not used to talking about his faith. The men listen. There are no women in this breakfast club. Jonathan reaches across and eats the sausage I have left on the side of my plate.

Graham finishes and is thanked by Tim. He suggests we might like to ask a few questions of the speaker. There is no response. An empty silence. I ask him a question about Christians in Sport, an organisation he has mentioned, just to ask something. He answers, then silence. Tim gets to his feet, offers thanks again for Graham's testament and then requests a five pound donation towards the breakfast.

I'm in Neath again. It is events that bring me home now. Tim has rung me in the week. He seems surprised that all his friends are coming back for the day, taking time off work.

The service is conducted by Alun Michael, Raymond's brother, a lay minister of god and enthusiasm. He asks for a celebration of Marlene's life and a thanks to God for her courage at the end. It had not been peaceful. The Mission chapel is as full as it can be. In a town of big funerals this is a very big funeral. I am late again and only find standing room at the back.

Tim and I used to go to this chapel together. Twenty five years ago, young boys reading from the Bible before being ushered into the Sunday school held in the annex. I resented my Sundays being taken away from me but I went. There were some good stories in the Bible: heroes, Gideon, David, Isaac. Names and stories were part of the firmament. Once a year we even had exams. I think I still have the certificates. The stories were told and we discussed them. And they were real hard stories of life in the desert. There seemed to be some disconnection in the church between the Old and the New Testament. A few years later and we were discussing the Holy Trinity – the teachers had difficulties with that one. But soon Ruskin's terrible hammers had moved ably into the hands of David Attenborough. There was no arguing with rocks and fossils. The Bible began to crumble, the society of the church only for me to question. At fourteen I decided not to go again. Tim persevered, remained within his faith which deepened.

We remained good friends, school, rugby, fishing and university tying your life with others who matter to you.

The singing starts. I listen carefully to the words. Halfway through the hymns I join in. I'd forgotten I actually like singing.

Marlene is buried in the council cemetery above the town. It is a beautiful day in October. A warm wind blows up the valley from the bay beyond. White clouds rush across the blue open sky. A crowd has gathered around the grave. They sing. I see the boys from the club, all in white shirts, wearing ties. Words are given freely to the wind, which hugs the people on the hill. I join a few words of the Lord's Prayer as it comes deeply from memory.

I watch Tim. He is careful to thank people for coming.

Aberteifi, 2002

Monday night on a train with the children and Gill. The miles again in the dark; just this bar, a few glasses of wine, café, and olives. Thinking about writing yet again. The darkness just beyond the window reminds me. I am close to this – too close to the depth of it all. Desire and life not easy companions on this journey through Spain.

The floor under the bar is thick with receipts, cigarette butts and empty packets of sugar. My little girl walks with me to the counter. I buy a glass of vino tinto. My pronunciation is good. As I sit down she tells me if I drink too much I will be drunk.

Gone from Under Your Nose

It is late summer. This year I'm living in a new town. A compact little town near the mouth of a river. It is not home. The hills are too small and we are too close to the sea. But I'm here with my family, a big house on the same street as the school and the swimming pool.

The rugby pitch is just up on the Aberystwyth road. It sits square in the town secured by space, a clubhouse and a stand. I've looked at it as I drive to the beach. Most days it is empty. Sometimes there's a couple of boys kicking a football around. There doesn't seem to be any sign of the team.

I read the first match reports in the paper. The team is off to a winning start. On the third Saturday of September I watch the Second team play Tenby. It is a close game on a hard ground. At half-time Cardigan make too many changes. Tenby stick to their team. They haven't brought any substitutes. Ten minutes into the second half Tenby have scored three tries as Cardigan fail to reorganise themselves with the new faces. The game is over. I watch the last thirty minutes. No-one knows me here. I have not brought my kit. I've packed it in. The last twenty years of weekly training and Saturday matches just stopped on a whim of age.

The smells come back to me. A crowded dressing room, deep heat, bandages. The rituals of preparation. Men joined in a community of ritual. Everyone knows their role, position, job.

There is a challenge to be met.

I remember a game late in the season when the referee made a statement to the changing room that he knew it was going to be a tough game but "Please nothing stupid, boys, we've all got work in the morning."

It is a game and more than a game. I was part of a club for twenty years. My father's name was on the captains' board in the 60's, my uncle's for a few seasons in the early 70's. My father had built the club – he was a builder and he put it up with a few mates on the weekends. To be part of the club was to be part of a society with its own rules. Traditions, memories, stories.

I had been taken to watch games as a six year old. My father was the coach by then. I didn't pay much attention but there was usually a wood next to the away ground where I could play and there was always faggots and peas and coke and crisps after the game.

I grew up with the game around. Uncles and cousins all played. It was in the paper, on the news. On international days we drew the heavy curtains of the living room and watched the tv. Then school. There was always a school team. I didn't enjoy it much. I was scared and unfit. The game hurt. There were boys with growth hormone problems who were six feet tall when the rest of us were five foot three. But it was part of me and I couldn't miss the challenge. All the teachers knew my father. I was expected to play.

In a tough valley we played the other schools. I remember losing 72 nil to Llangatwg when tries were worth four points and they didn't bother kicking conversions. The sheer terror of trying to catch a ball with the big, hairy, surely overage forwards massing on the far side, only ten short yards away. At least at school the opposition were likely to be the same age. In club rugby the under 13 front row for Seven Sisters were all shaving.

We eventually caught up with Llangatwg as we produced a hormone success of our own in the shape of Lyndon Jones. A fierce bull of a fifteen year old boy, Lyndon was known to turn up for a Saturday morning game after a heavy night of drinking on the town. He was often covered in love bites and once, before a Sevens tournament in Hereford, produced a used condom out of the pocket of his duffel coat. At fifteen I had never seen a condom or kissed a girl. There seemed more chance of a trip to the moon.

The fear of seeing Lyndon Jones, all six foot fourteen stone of him running towards me on a training field finally receded a few months later when he fell over me in my attempt to get out of his way. The games teacher, Dai Will, shouted "Good tackle, Richard" and I realised if you put enough bulk in front of something it will usually stop them.

I tried this ten years later, trying to stop Dale Mackintosh, a monstrous but friendly New Zealander playing for Pontypridd. The club still owes me the dental bills. You've got to tackle forward not backwards.

School moved to youth rugby – a whole new set of rules. Older boys – still boys – and better singing, more drinking. Wales has a culture of youth that is centred on drinking. How much you can drink before falling over is seen as an attainment. This pervades all rugby in Wales and youth rugby was soaked in it.

At this point in life I didn't enjoy alcohol. I made a point of avoiding it. I was the only rugby player in the team who didn't drink. This lasted a year. I'm not sure about the standard of the rugby but my drinking improved.

And then rugby is a process of growing up and leaving. I had a few choices given by education. To leave Wales and study in London. I played for London Welsh in an under 21 team of New Zealanders, Englishmen, Australians, South Africans and a vague north Walian. It was great rugby. I made some good friends in six months with boys I have never seen again.

Somehow I returned home after university. I got a job on a building site with my father. I was back playing with the same boys who had been in the school and then youth team. We were older. Just a few years. Most of us played for the second team.

There were men in the first team. Men thirty years old with muscles, real muscles and a toughness that comes with ten years of hard labour or ten years of just playing rugby on a Saturday afternoon. The men had wives and children. Some already bore some of the scars. You can get hurt playing against men.

I can go on with this but it is my story. One of thousands. I wrote a book about it. Losing, winning. My concerns at the time, work, sex and rugby.

It is the moments that stay with you. The days in the rain. A high ball caught running backwards towards the post against New Dock Stars. Finally winning away against Banwen, shouting to myself as I drove out of the village on a Saturday night after the game, elation. A dummy which sent me in under the posts against Tonna Seconds. Running out under lights for Pontypridd, the big time, the first xv. One game. Phil Vaughan congratulating me in the Bryncoch clubhouse after winning a game against Seven Sisters. Phil Vaughan was and is a hero of mine. Winning and losing. There are deep pleasures in victory, despair in losing but you have to know both.

The final few years of playing, a synthesis of ideas. New directions, clearing the mind on a Saturday afternoon. Anything to play. The same joke every week in the showers. The men before us on the touchlines, the boys grown into men. Something in being part of the tribe. Sunday mornings always stiff with bruises, feeling alive. To play is it all.

Then it is gone from under your nose.

Aberteifi, 2003

Tonight it is dark. I watch the water and the lights pass below the window. The boat is still but moving. Outside I look back into Barcelona. I am covered by ash. Black ash from the guts of the ship as the engine warms up. I check twice to make sure it is ash. It must be a joke but the ash keeps falling.

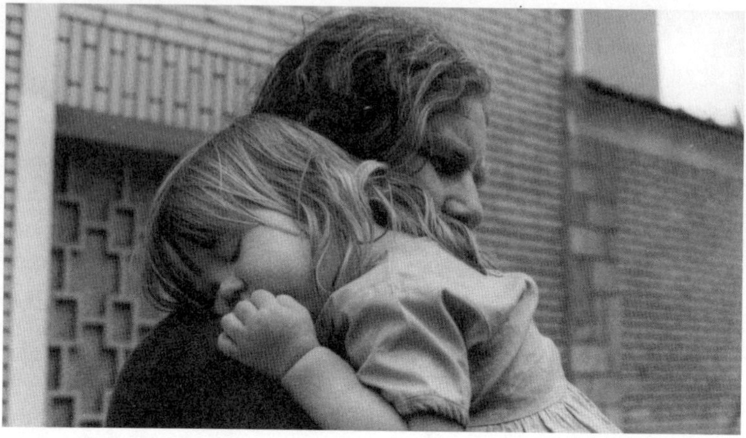

Pieces of Happiness 1989-2003

My Piece of Happiness has been a process of change and collaboration. A first draft of a work that would have several forms was written over a bank holiday weekend in May 1992. Eight years later, a finished novel was launched with a reading at Waterstone's Bookshop at the Hayes in Cardiff. As the writer whose name appears on the spine of the book, I think of the book as mine but it is not mine. The work has had a life and experience beyond my input and as the book which sits on the shelves is bought, read and reviewed, it will have others. The story will continue.

Eight years in development appears now to be a long time. *My Piece of Happiness* is my third novel and fourth published book.

In *For Love and Money* Jonathan Raban captured the balance of possibilities for the writer attempting to live by and through his writing. It is a thoughtful book on the nature of living through writing.

"I've written out of compulsion, for love, and I've needed the money."

But this delicious balance is only afforded to the successful writer. The writer who does not sell his work does not have the luxury of balancing love and money. There is only love. This does not mean that writers who receive no money for their work have been unsuccessful in their writing, just that they have not been able to make any money from it. The writers who have made money from their work have always been successful. Someone has paid money for it. In *Goodbye to All That*, Robert Graves comments that "The indirect proceeds from poem-writing can be enormously higher than the direct ones." He had just been appointed as a 25-year-old professor of poetry at Alexandria University. It was his first teaching appointment.

In 1997 the Arts Council of England in association with Waterstone's published a book entitled *The Cost of Letters* (subtitled *How much do you think a writer needs to live on?*), introduced by Alain de Botton and based on Cyril Connolly's 1946 editor's questionnaire for the magazine *Horizon*. The book was a series of responses by a range of mostly well-known and predominantly London-based writers to a series of questions under the broad heading of the title. The writers who responded used skills in evasion and deception, largely avoiding the subtext of the questionnaire, which was to reveal the answer to the question "How much do you live on?" Most of them were able to discuss the question well in the abstract but completely avoided the practical reality. Other writers, they said, could well live on anything from six to eighteen thousand a year, but the balance of their own personal finances remained a mystery. Writers are perhaps afraid of delving too closely into the source of their income in case the mysterious equation of money and life for words disappears as suddenly as it appeared. There are also tax claims and former partners to consider. The life of a freelance writer is only viable according to their current ability, contacts, luck. Speak too much about it and the charms with which you surround yourself disappear.

There are no salaries for people making a living out of writing books, plays and television programmes. There are rates, but they are only guidelines, and to get the rates you have got to get the work.

For me, living by my writing has always appealed to a notion of freedom that you can never really abandon. "The idea of living in London and writing for a living – writing anything for a living – possessed me completely. Every morning was distinctly brighter because of the idea." (Jonathan Raban, *For Love and Money*) I have now given up my ambitions of playing rugby for Wales, but I still think I can make a living out of writing.

I arrived in Cardiff in the Autumn of 1989 with the idea of completing a collection of short stories before proceeding to law school. I managed to convince the administrators of the Swansea enterprise allowance scheme that my outline for six short stories was a viable commercial consideration. I would write them over a year and sell them to a publisher. They duly advanced me a grant of £40 per week. It was also possible to claim housing benefit on the basis of low income, and I was able to rent a room in a house on Colum Road. Nine months later I had completed a collection of short stories.

They Promised £40 A Week

It seemed like a good idea, joining Margaret's enterprise economy. They promised forty pounds a week. I only had to produce some original words. There were a few preconditions. I had to be claiming for six weeks. I was over-qualified for that one. Then there was the induction day, eight hours of how to run a successful business. I even took a notepad. My fellow conspirators eyed me as I scribbled. I'm a writer, I explained. Obviously, they concluded. But there was the free lunch; my first. Then the thousand quid. But the bank provided an overdraft. They were giving them away then. Weeks later a letter. They said yes and offered a Monday in June. I said summer and wanted a Thursday in October. We compromised.

September and a new flat in a new city. A new start, said my mother. A new night out, said my mind. But I have to write, you can only visit the museum so many times. I write, then I read: books, then papers, then the mail. It's not mine but I read it anyway. A postcard from Weymouth. Matthew likes it there. Would I like Matthew? Probably not if he likes Weymouth. There's an offer for Mr Broome. A dictionary of all the world's Broomes. It's only forty nine pounds including postage and packing.

I don't get much mail. I like it that way. Nobody knows I'm here except the rebate cheque, but then it's followed by a tax assessment. I don't need to hide the figures.

Three months in, my first draft is sitting on the floor but I'm on holiday. It is Christmas and there's a film on in the afternoon. I'm writing now, it's a new line and it's working well.

New Year's a downer. Broome arrives for his mail. I lie. There's legal proceedings for Malik. Should I be doing this? Money's short and I'm out of books. I offer to review. There's a letter. It's a rejection but good practice. I'm summoned by Margaret. They want a report on their investment. I could be delivering pizzas and they would never know. I turn up with a sheaf of A4, yellowing around the edges with filtered beer. It's a Neath trait. I can't always find the pan. She fingers it reluctantly. Everything else okay? We will contact you again. They never do.

Spring arrives with whiskey, a party and a girl I shouldn't have kissed. A manuscript and a typescript and three weeks on a roof. There's good money in slates. The post is expensive, the wait longer. Faber thank but say no. I post again. Seren don't like the punctuation. Neither do I. But there's still the grand. I catch a train to Morocco.

I wrote *They promised £40 per week* at the end of the year. It had been a good year. I had written. Not very much, looking at it now. But there was a glimpse of a future there.

After returning from Morocco I realised the literary life was going to be a bit more difficult than I imagined. I saw a job advertisement for work with the Small Scale Day Service. The Day Service was a department of South Glamorgan Social Services working with adults with learning difficulties. Its main remit was to provide support to enable people to stay in their family homes or reintegrate back into society after prolonged periods of institutional care. It was the summer of 1990. My literary career had lasted nine months but at least I knew I wasn't going to study law.

The job allowed me to work at a novel at least four nights a week. I had started a book about a young labourer/builder who is frustrated with his life but can't see a way out of his routine existence.

I manage to work on the book consistently for a year. I make attempts to get it published but there were no offers. The Bridgend-based publisher Seren Books claim there is not enough interest in the narrative but offer to read my next book. A fierce reader's report from an agent in London suggests it is completely unpublishable. I continue writing.

The part-time post for the Day Service merges into a full-time salaried position for South Glamorgan Social Services. I am contracted to work 37 hours a week, but this has the great advantage of being the exact number of hours I actually work. There is no overtime, and I do not take work home with me. A year, then another, passes quickly. I continue writing. I try a few more short stories and run thirty thousand words into a comic novel set in Cardiff Bay. The work is building, but from the outside I seem to be making no progress.

After three years of writing I still have nothing published. Cardiff as a city has opened possibilities of other forms of writing. I have begun watching productions of new work at the Sherman theatre. Made In Wales stage a retrospective of the work of Alan Osborne which fills the theatre while a play by Mike Kenny on Dylan Thomas convinces me I can write dialogue. If I can write dialogue, I reason, I can write a play.

I decide to give up the job for Social Services and write a play about the people and the work instead. It is a step out into insecurity with no prospect of an income, but I have no other responsibilities and I want to write. I want to learn how to write and for that I need time. Again, words from Jonathan Raban quoting Larkin in *For Love and Money*

"I had Larkin's lines in my head.
> *Ah, were I courageous enough to shout Stuff your pension!*
> *But I know, all too well, that's the stuff that dreams are made on...*
But it's not, and it wasn't."

I quit work early due to a broken leg sustained in a rugby match and begin work on editing the novel. Then, beginning on a long bank holiday weekend, I write two plays in three weeks.

It is the second holiday of summer. The weather is warm and there is snooker on the TV. I hide myself away at a desk on the east side of the house. It is cooler and the sun is high over the slates by the time I begin work. The words come easy. I know what I want to say and have a rough idea how to put my words across. The scenes unfold easily, quickly, out of each other. I am in a rush to write them. I pause briefly after each burst of scene to sit in the garden and watch the summer catch up with itself before returning to the desk, my pen and a rapidly filling pad of A4 paper. It is one of the finest feelings as a writer to be inside an idea when it is going well and the words want to be said. I can remember the heat and the words and the cups of tea and Gill sitting in the garden reading. It is a fine time.

I feel it is important to be happy when writing. I see no point in being otherwise. I enjoy the life I lead.

"There were times when you had to write. Not conscience. Just peristaltic action. It was really more fun than anything else...." Nick Adams in "Big Two Hearted River" by Ernest Hemingway

Within six weeks I had two plays as typescripts. They looked like plays. I chose titles, bought envelopes and more paper and began mailing copies of the plays to any theatre company listed in the *Writers' Handbook* that claimed to produce new work.

Summer Optimism

I had enough money to last out the summer before spending a winter in India. Rent had been cheap in Cardiff; I had saved money for a trip abroad, somewhere warm, somewhere I could live on £60 a week. I had not sold a single word of my work. The urge to continue writing was an idea fuelled by the need to write, ambition and the optimism of confidence. I had written one novel, one collection of short stories, and two plays. All unpublished or unproduced.

The winter of 1992 passed with one sale, *My Wales*, Dutch auctioned for twenty quid to the Tenby Tourist Board for a piece on a Sunday school trip to the town. I still remember the elation of receiving the cheque through the post. I have never read the words in print. Another story from work that winter appeared in *Cambrensis*, the short story magazine. There was no payment, only two free copies of the magazine for publication. This again was optimism overcoming reality.

I returned to Cardiff in March 1993. I had no money, no immediate prospect of a job and had abandoned the novel set in Cardiff Bay. In India and later Australia I had written only diaries and letters but I had written every day. It had provided practice, the actual action of writing. In addition I had been reading two books a week. A diary entry from that winter reveals how travel can have unexpected benefits for a writer.

Travelling a strange game. The multitude of experiences which consume your ordinary life – friends, work, meetings, sport, cinema – are suddenly removed, pared down to the basic view of the traveller. New sights, strange people and places, but more ordinarily sitting in cafes, waiting in queues for tickets to keep the momentum going; reading time expands considerably as the tv suddenly holds no interest.

In *On Writing*, Stephen King claims to be reading around seventy books a year. One early offer of advice to the writer is based on a story from his childhood where with the encouragement of his brother and a class science project he succeeds in blowing up his tv and short-circuiting a whole block of flats. He considers the end of a reliance on television as entertainment to be crucial in releasing time and action for the writer. Although there are many interesting programmes on tv it is a leech on time and action. I lost the habit during a winter in India. I still occasionally watch it in the houses of friends but I do not own one.

Writing is a need but also a pleasure, and the release of travel provides plenty to consider and write about. But on return I still had to face the reality that I was a writer with no published book.

The first novel still sat in a cupboard in my parents' house. It was a time to stay in touch with dreams.

In Times Like These

It is 1993. I am drinking with Ravi at a pub in Cardiff. A poetry reading has just finished. The pub is half-empty but begins to fill up as more invited guests arrive to eat the buffet. I am not invited to the buffet but as no-one moves to throw me out I take a plastic plate and begin stacking it with sandwiches and crisps. The poet looks around as the crowd increases and wonders why they didn't turn up an hour earlier. I introduce myself to Topher Mills. He's just returned a novel of mine from his Red Sharks imprint. He stands out from the crowd in a big red blazer. He explains that Red Sharks only publish poetry, but perhaps I should set up a company myself, maybe a cooperative? I fill another plate from the Academy buffet. The Literature Festival is over.

Parthian Books published my first novel in September 1993. I had set up the company with a loan from the Prince's Youth Business Trust and another Enterprise Allowance grant. The business was based on two books, *Work, Sex and Rugby* and *How To Publish Yourself,* a manual on self-publishing by Peter Finch. I had spent six months researching the business while finishing the text of the novel.

I had written a couple of books, but without finding a publisher it would have been a long struggle to convince myself I should have done something else for a living.
    Words from an article I wrote on writing for the Academi magazine, *A470*

I considered that the novel I had written was worth reading. I was going to make sure that it could be read. The publishing company had a business plan and a product, *Work, Sex and Rugby*. The book sold, the title ensured publicity while word of mouth and good reviews did the rest. In terms of Welsh publishing, it was a success. There was money from writing. Not much, and most came from publishing. On its first print run *WSR* sold 2000 copies at a cover price of £4.99. At a royalty of 10% this produced £998 for the author. Two years' work. Without also owning the publishing company, the author would again be working at a deficit. But for an author working as a publisher the book paid for itself and accumulated a small surplus. I paid myself £40 a week. Subsequently the publishing company has expanded to publish a further 40 titles, becoming the leading contemporary fiction publisher in Wales. It has its own independence from and dependence on the work of Lewis Davies as a publisher and a writer, (*WSR* is its best selling title with over 7000 copies sold to date) but at the beginning of 1994 Parthian had only published one book, which was out of stock.

In Wales there are other avenues of support for writers who are considered to be producing work of some literary merit. The Arts Council of Wales at that time provided bursaries tax-free for the purpose of buying time for writers. With *WSR* riding a surge of good reviews I applied for and received a bursary. I had applied for between £4000 and £6000 based on a projected income of between £8000 and £12000. I received £4000. This I planned would last a year at least. During the winter of 1994/5 I first retreated to mid-Wales to write *Tree of Crows*. I was living in a cottage in a field. As the winter set in I wrote a short manuscript. I remember the place as cold and wet, caught in a deep valley and wishing for the sun. Late in January I gave up on the half-finished book and fled to Sri Lanka. The country was warm, light and filled with the possibilities of the tropics. I had brought several manuscripts to finish. The second draft of the play, *My Piece of Happiness*, rejected again by the readers of Made in Wales and a number of London theatres, looking thin and gutted by its recent treatment, appeared at my table on the verandah. I had attempted to interest a number of theatre companies in producing the play and although the reports looked promising and the script had even gone to committee stage at the Royal Court, no-one had invited me in to discuss the work. I was outside looking in. I was in Sri Lanka.

During March and April 1995 in a six week run I worked on *My Piece of Happiness* every morning between 9 and 12, writing prose from the dialogue of the script. At the end I had an early draft of a short novel. I had resolved that if *My Piece of Happiness* was not going to get produced as a play it would appear as a novel. I was buoyed by the success of *WSR* and full of the confidence an artist has when he controls the means of production. Without control the artist can be emasculated and eventually suffocated. There is nothing as overwhelming as the desert of apathy that can be lavished on the production of a new work.

"Any writer, I suppose, feels that the world into which he was born is nothing less than a conspiracy against the cultivation of his talent – which attitude certainly has a great deal to support it. On the other hand, it is only because the world looks on his talent with such frightening indifference that the artist is compelled to make his talent important."
Notes of a Native Son, James Baldwin

In *Notes of a Native Son*, James Baldwin claims that it is this indifference that motivates the great artists to produce works of significance. But there is a limit to the number of productions an artist can force through this frightening silence.

My Piece of Happiness had moved from being *A Place for Sean* during the summer of 1994. I had changed the title after listening to a young woman with learning difficulties claim she had a right to her own "piece of happiness". It suited the themes of the play as they were developing, and as I realised that the novel was not just about Sean but each individual character's search for happiness. Now it was shaping into a new form. The novel afforded more space for the characters to roam around the city that had become very definitely Cardiff. I was also able to return to a few of the characters that had been removed in the second re-write. I had reacted to suggestions from the reports commissioned by Made In Wales. They wanted fewer characters. This is a difficult area to approach for inexperienced writers. Everyone will have a view on your work. Unless people have an empathy for your work, it is better to discount their suggestions and stick to what you believe in. The problem of a commissioned reader's report is particularly acute. Readers for tv and theatre companies are usually out-of-work writers filling in time between commissions. Only the very best are objective; the rest are a mixed bag of prejudices and insecurity. The prospect of receiving a useful report in this context is problematic. Poor scripts are easy to reject, better scripts are always a threat. The scripts that do receive good reports usually concur with the writer's worldview but are probably less polished and therefore no threat. Praise can be just as dangerous in these circumstances as condemnation. It might be better to discount all anonymous reports but inevitably you can't. As a writer you must read and react to them.

The Pitch

Writing is only part of the process of getting a work produced, performed, published.

I had sent the play first to the Royal Court. It is the premier new writing theatre in the country and has an international reputation. My first completed play, *Waiting for the Fall*, based on the closure of a mine my grandfather worked and died in, had reached the committee stage at the Court and they had asked to see my next completed work. *Happiness* had a good reception, went again to committee stage and then was sent back to me with a report. Then nothing. No follow up, no invitation to a workshop, no correspondence with a writer who could obviously write drama but was just as clearly unused to the theatre. I was outside looking in.

I continued sending the play to a series of theatres committed to new writing. I received a variety of responses, mostly positive. Artistic directors went out of their way to claim merits for the work without offering any further suggestions on how it was going to be produced. Looking at these letters now, I feel a sense of lost opportunity but also frustration and some anger. The Made in Wales reports were perhaps the worst at offering encouragement without back-up.

The company was funded by the Arts Council of Wales to develop and produce work by new writers. In three years they provided six reader's reports of varying quality and finally a letter from the artistic director, Gilly Adams, suggesting I might like to take part in a workshop at some time in the future. This is a terrible inertia to overcome for a writer trying to get a stage play produced and learn about the theatre.

One report from Made In Wales even lead with the reader's own opinions on the nature of sexuality between people who have learning difficulties. It is an attitude the play tries to confront head on. From this point the reader has fixed his/her reaction and wilfully misunderstands/ignores the drama, hence the argument, within the play. As a writer I needed to move past or ignore these receptions. You cannot argue with them since they are on the page and the reports are anonymous. But there was hope within the pages of comment, snatches of recognition and engagement. "I would encourage you to keep going as you have within your grasp the potential to explore worlds and lives we haven't experienced before" – The Bush Theatre. "It is a brave play asking essential questions about care, love, responsibility, and happiness. I don't feel it is ready for production as yet, but is certainly worth developing as a script. "– Rose Sharp at the Gay Sweatshop. The report from the Gay Sweatshop was poignant in that it asked about the characters, that now at the second major draft, lived only off stage. Reacting to the first run of reports from Made In Wales I had shortened the play. This was completely the wrong approach. It needed expanding and focusing.

But then there is the final short postcard from Gilly Adams, a throwaway invitation that she never followed up and the comments from her reader's report, to fire me on or stop me writing. "As with the other play of his I read he seems not to have given it enough time as though he doesn't take himself seriously." This, even now, makes me angry.

The reports I received give a snapshot of the amount of effort required to move on with the words that you believe in.

They give an account of the progress of a play that was unlikely ever to get produced.

1995

1995 was a long year of nothing for my own work. I arrived back from Sri Lanka in early summer with a travel book, two novels that needed more work and no means of earning a living. I was soon back on the building site. It would be a year before *Tree of Crows* was published. I wrote in spare time at the weekends or in the weeks when it rained. I wrote another two plays, both of which got promising but inconclusive responses from theatres in London. But *My Piece of Happiness* was going to get another life. The artistic directorship of Made in Wales had changed. Jeff Teare, a former director of new writing at Stratford East Theatre in London had been appointed to the post with a remit of producing new, diverse work. During the autumn I sent copies of my two new plays, both returned in the same week of January 1996. Mr Teare had written short, positive, if rather terse, appraisals of both, responding to the readers' reports he had commissioned. I was fed up of these reports. I sent the second draft of *My Piece of Happiness* with the suggestion that he might like to read it himself.

A couple of months later Jeff invited me into the Made In Wales office. They were in preparation for production and an air of expectancy filled the room. He'd read the play. I presented him with the draft of the novel version which had resurrected the missing characters, and he invited me to submit the play for a workshop that would take place during a season of new plays at The Point in Cardiff Bay.

I took a week off from the building work in the third week of September. The theatre was quiet in the morning. It was a ten o'clock call and the actors arrived in small groups, talking amongst themselves. There was a world here, and I was once again looking in. But I was inside the theatre. Jeff Teare introduced me and the play. The actors read from the script: the words worked. I could hear them. I can see the faces and the people as they enjoyed themselves with the new words and dropped the subtle introductions to sentences that you don't need on the stage. I marked my script in pencil with notes and suggestions from Jeff. The lay-out was all wrong. Two words the same on consecutive lines chime like a bell. The structure, well; the structure was too big a topic to begin discussing today.

We try a final read through for a few friends who have turned up: Gill Griffiths, Simon Day, Eve Piffaretti, Alan Osborne. The words run again. Then the actors and Jeff call it off for lunch.

We eat at Buff's, a wine bar in the docks catering for business men. Jeff talks to me and says he thought the reading went well. "We'll bung you a couple of hundred and see how things go on the rewrite." I take his arm off.

The walk home is a fine afternoon in the rain. Alan Osborne accompanies me. He is a playwright who has had a long association with Made in Wales, two or three big productions and a full retrospective of his work. He is generous in his assessment of the play and its ambitions. We walk up along Taff Embankment, stopping at the Inn on the River, drifting through the landscape of the story. I drink a few pints but at this stage I am drunk on elation. I believe absolutely that this play will see a production.

Collaboration, words, people, love

Writing the words that you love are bound up with all aspects of your life. They are not something that can be separated out into their own constituencies. *My Piece of Happiness* is a work of collaboration. Gill Griffiths, my partner of ten years, has had a direct influence on all of my work since reading the first two chapters of *WSR*. We met while working together for Social Services. As such she had a personal understanding of the world of *My Piece of Happiness*. She is an artist who exhibits her own work. She is also a considered critic of contemporary writing.

I can see her tears while she sits in the garden of her house in Skelmuir Road and reads the play for the first time. She has been the first reader of all my work and is both critic and muse. She will comment candidly and effectively on any aspect of my writing. I am more likely to respond to her suggestions or criticisms than anyone else's.

The first reading of the play is an important moment for both of us. It is part of the confirmation of this life we lead and have chosen together. She has directly influenced *WSR* by reading it, *Tree of Crows* by sharing a cottage with me while I was writing it, *Freeways: A Journey West on Route 66*, by being in it. The book is dedicated to Martha, an Australian hitch hiker the writer/narrator picks up on the road west out of New Mexico. The narrator has an affair with Martha before being dumped in favour of her long term boyfriend, Byron, on the sidewalk in Las Vegas. It forms the central section of the book and leads directly into the story of Steinbeck, *The Grapes of Wrath* and the migrant farm workers which is the core of the story. Martha is Gill.

I had been awarded the *Freeways* commission by the John Morgan Writing Trust. Again on the back of *WSR* I had applied for their annual award for a generous travel writing prize. I had submitted a proposal about islands in the Irish sea. The committee had liked my work but felt I needed more ambition in my proposal. Jo Menell, the trustee who financially supported the award rang me up on a Friday evening and suggested I come up with something better by Monday. Six months earlier I had read *The Grapes of Wrath*. I had also been reading news reports about migrant workers in California. I was interested in the need to travel for work, in the search for roots and, finally, in Steinbeck. As I read more about Steinbeck the source of his inspiration and collaboration became clear. But the man also shifted. You can know too much about a writer.

John Steinbeck is a writer who depended on and directly collaborated with his wife, Carol, on all his books up to *The Grapes of Wrath*. The book is dedicated to her and Tom Collins. "For Carol who willed it and Tom who lived it," ten words that recognise and hide the contribution of two writers to one of the most revered books in American literature. Tom Collins was a migrant camp manager in the San Joaquin Valley in the 1930s; a writer himself, he was able to show Steinbeck his notebooks on migrant worker life which included dialogue extracts and some short stories. Steinbeck initially proposed a collaboration with Collins on a documentary style book on migrant labour. Steinbeck's editor, Pat Covici, persuaded the author that a novel would make more sense, and over three years Steinbeck pulled away from a full collaboration. But he kept the notebooks. Carol Steinbeck always typed her husband's laborious first longhand draft into copy. She edited as she wrote. Steinbeck needed this control and influence. They burnt one 60,000 word manuscript that preceded *The Grapes of Wrath* because they knew the next book would be better. Steinbeck completed his book in one long draft that was immediately edited and typed by his wife. They finished it together in the fall of 1938, Carol finding the title from a line in *The Battle Hymn of the Republic* late in the production of the manuscript.

"To Carol who willed it..."

The Grapes of Wrath, when finally published, overwhelmed and finally wrecked the Steinbeck's marriage. John had lost his collaborator. *The Grapes of Wrath* seemed to exhaust him as a writer and change him as a person. In a few years he went from an author who shunned publicity because it interrupted his work, to lunching with the President of the United States and offering him suggestions on domestic policy. He moved to New York with a new wife and lost his reasons for writing.

In 1943 he wrote a book for the war effort, *The Moon is Down*. Ernest Hemingway was direct in his appraisal when he commented that he'd rather cut off two fingers of his pitching hand than write such work.

Hemingway needed his wives more and less. Hadley Richardson provided early stability, a shared love of the world and a private income which sustained them in their Paris years. Pauline Pfeiffer provided a larger income but little understanding of his work. Martha Gellhorn provided competition and escape from Pauline. Mary Welsh provided tolerance and someone to grow old with, but it was to Hadley he returned in his work in the late sentimental *A Moveable Feast*, regretting the "pilot fish" Dos Passos who brought Pauline into a world of happiness.

I need Gill Griffiths for myself and for my work. She has provided a stability, sometimes emotional, sometimes financial, that allows time to live and create.

The fullest expression of this is the story "Mr Roopratna's Chocolate". It was written about our visit to Sri Lanka during the spring of 1995. We were staying in a village called Unawatuna on the south coast near Galle, while I was working on *My Piece of Happiness* and *Freeways*. The narrator of the story is a painter hiding from the European winter while struggling to fill large expressionist canvases. Gill has provided expressionist paintings for all my books to date, except *Freeways*, for which she provided the photographs. She exhibited these photographs at the Dylan Thomas Centre, Tŷ Llen, Swansea during the summer of 1996, a year before the publication of the book. I have become accustomed to using her work as inspiration and a medium for discussion. The painter in "Mr Roopratna's Chocolate" is Gill and he/she is also me. But again it is neither of us, an expression of memory and time seen through the fictional prism.

Support for me also means family. My mother and father

have had an influence on my writing, both financial and emotional. I am aware I have been fortunate and that my parents are patient.

"The reason I have not sent you any of my work is because you or Mother sent back the *In Our Time* books. That looked as though you did not want to see any."

Ernest Hemingway in a letter to his father. Paris, 20th March, 1925.

My parents are not regular readers. My father has read all my work. I'm not sure if my mother has read any of my books. Direct questions on the subject provide vague replies. But they are firm supporters of my endeavours. My father has provided irregular employment on building sites when the flow of words for money has been ephemeral. Cash flow problems have often been cash droughts. They are both investors in Parthian Books and have acted as an effective local sales force for books and play tickets. I sometimes have the feeling that they would both prefer me to have a regular job. My appearance on my father's building site after a university education created bewilderment and a raw unaired panic. Education was supposed to be about getting a job so that I didn't need to go on the building site.

Eighteen months of labouring provided me with enough material for my first novel, but it didn't feel like research at the time. They both now understand more of what I am trying to do and how I live my life. My father has been self-employed all his life. He understands the freedom and insecurity of living on your ability. My mother is captured by the words in George Brinley Evans's story *Boys Of Gold*:

"Owen was looking at [his] mother, looking at her eyes. Looking for what only a son can see in the eyes of his mother. And no man ever born has seen it any other place. In that instant of light, you bask, you bathe; you become the boy of pure gold."

My parents' support has been tempered with questions and firm, considered advice, but it has always been unconditional.

Re-writes

I write the next re-draft of the play quickly. The day after the reading. It is essential to begin when the words of the actors are still fresh in my mind. I take three working days to produce a new draft. Working days involve starting at nine in the morning and working until one. The afternoons are not for writing.

Alun Richards recalls a meeting with Kurt Vonnegut at the Tokyo Book Fair when the writer suggested to a packed audience that the biggest problem facing the successful writer was what to do with the afternoons.

I stop for a few minutes when a scene has been completed, but apart from that it is important to write straight through a period of concentrated work. Early the following week a draft is ready for delivery. I read through a printed draft twice, make some changes and some editing corrections. The play is back close to its original form with a couple of new scenes between Sarah, Sean's girlfriend, and her mother. I wait a respectable two weeks before posting it back to Made in Wales. There is a wait of a further couple of weeks before Jeff invites me back down to the office. The excitement of the season is fading and it is a long run until the next play, which will appear in the spring. The office is more tattered, somehow worn by the rush of people who have all now dispersed to their own lives after sharing a few sharp weeks together. Jeff offers me a contract and sort of apologizes that it is only an equity minimum of £4500 payable in three instalments. I wave away and towards the thought of the money. It is a commission from a professional theatre company. Someone else is putting serious money into the development of my work. More than that they are putting their own professional interest into words and people that I have created on the page. A commission is no guarantee of production but I have no doubt that Made in Wales will stage the show. And finally £4500 sounds like a lot of money.

Jeff's comment on the rewrite is that the characters tend to "jump up on us". I take this to mean that we need to move more slowly into their worlds, which of course means longer scenes and more words. I rewrite again quickly, I know I must catch the enthusiasm and life of the moment before I am absorbed by new work, publishing and the rush of the winter.

My writing is beginning to be published again, with *Tree of Crows* launched in the first week of October by Parthian. The company is expanding. It also publishes a prize-winning Welsh language novel in translation and an award winning screenplay. It is essentially a cooperative, but I assume the role of front man and main sales agent. The books sell well, though without the rush that followed the first novel. But now I have a commission. I reckon I can last on £2000 well into the following spring if I'm careful. I do not need this to write but just to live. I have finished my work on the play until the next reading.

A New Reading

We meet in the cafe at Chapter. It is 10am on a Tuesday morning in February 1997. Ten copies of the play are waiting on the table for the actors, stage manager, director, assistant director and writer. Jeff and I have already discussed what we are doing. At least Jeff knows what he is doing. Only one of the actors, James Westaway remains from the first read through. James will play Sean, the young man at the centre of the play. I am keen that Lowri should play Sean's girlfriend, Sarah but she unavailable for the reading. However both Sharon Morgan and Dorien Thomas are available for a one day reading. It's fifty quid for a few hours work. I know that they will do the play. Jeff has talked about how the process of developing a play benefits enormously if the writer has an idea of the strengths of the actors who will eventually interpret the roles. We'll need five actors for the final production. I am now writing for four of them. David Middleton will not appear until the final casting, but his ability to interpret four varying roles will be crucial. There are ten characters in the play.

The reading goes well. There are rehearsal room laughs and plenty of discussion about the characters and their motivation. I'm not sure what I learn from it. I feel the actors enjoy themselves, but then they always do. In the early evening we discuss other plays in the backroom of The Butchers Arms. It is a dreary pub but Dorien seems to be comfortable there. I will try to avoid it in future.

I begin to think the play is ready. I have underwritten so there is not much room for cutting. The only problem is length and the chimera of structure, which everyone has a theory on, but no-one really understands. I spend another few mornings re-writing using notes made in the rehearsal. The production had been planned for the autumn but Jeff has bumped it back a few months to January 1998. At first I am disappointed. But the winter produces other considerations. Gill is pregnant and a blond and strident baby boy arrives in the first days of March.

This is a new time. I have other responsibilities, but I am living by my writing. The boy produces a surge of activity, but I have tried to finish my re-writing by March, and during the first few months I have no new work that I need to finish.

The publishing again consumes my writing time. Parthian produces *Freeways: A Journey West On Route 66* by Lewis Davies. It is a name I have grown accustomed to now. The book has somehow become finished between the plays and the second novel. I am in a hurry to get it published, maybe too much of a hurry, but the reviews and eventually the sales are good. I have experimented with tense structure in the narrative, which is a mixture of fact and fiction. The style gets some criticism for uneven reading. There is safety and clarity within one tense. However, experimenting does afford different opportunities within the realism of narrative. The flow of life and words do not occur in one tense and framework. The entrainment of life on the road is reflected in the prose of *Freeways*. It is a technique I will return to.

The early autumn sees a final discussion on the structure and strengths of *My Piece of Happiness*. Jeff still wants more words, and I conjure another scene between Sean and Sarah. It will become the scene at the beginning of the second act. I begin to believe that I really know these characters, and other scenes suggest themselves without being written. We still seem a long way from production, but the cast is fixed. We do not hold auditions. Jeff is riding high on the success of *Gulp* by Roger Williams, and the company is on a roll. The office has moved to Chapter Arts Centre, which becomes the focus of new Welsh theatre for a few months.

The story now has another life, the life of the novel it will become. Parthian submits the short manuscript for consideration for an Arts Council publication grant. I have not worked on the prose version since being in Sri Lanka, but it is readable and gets conditional recommendations from two anonymous readers. It needs more work, more development, more resolution. The advantage of unpublished constructive criticism is that, if you agree with it, you can also do something about it. The novel would have to wait until more time presented itself, but a basis existed to complete the book.

This is also an anonymous reader's report, but I listen to it. It is about the book, its strengths and weaknesses and what it could be. Too many reports are about the author of the report and their opinions on drama/literature. I perceive that the reader has thought about the book and what it requires in terms of development and changes. It is also crucial that I agree with it. I know the book needs more work. Criticism is a difficult medium to get accustomed to, but it is inherent in any discussion of literature. Everyone has their own ideas.

And within this life there was another: the doctorate in creative writing. The discussion of the art, the process of practice, disturbing less the subtle skills slip away under too close an analysis.

"There is one part of writing that is solid and you do no harm by talking about it, the other is fragile, and if you talk about it, the structure cracks and you have nothing."
Ernest Hemingway in conversation with George Plimpton, *Paris Review*

I was completing a number of short stories for discussion. The work I was submitting was often close to completion: a few more sentences, a refinement of form, polishing a fourth or fifth draft of a story only three thousand words. A whole world within a few pages. The crucial words at the end of a week's work that make a story complete. I finished five in the year. Snapshots of time, resurrected drafts of ideas on paper that were now becoming stories. I was trying for more length, more structure, less obvious meanings in a sequence of works that I had culled from a few years of travelling and city observation: "This Time of Year"; a young man on a building site killed by falling scaffolding; "Tom's Castle", two sales representatives trying to get laid at the London Book Fair; "Feeding the House Crows", a traveller in India robbed of all his belongings and having to face the country for the first time; "When the Woman Sings", a lonely woman taking part in a carnival so she can eat and drink with strangers; "Mr Roopratna's Chocolate", an artist in Sri Lanka, wasting away the winter while trying to speak to the estate gardener in broken Sinhalese. None of these stories had to be written. They were stories to write. But the worlds they created led me into them again and again. Three were built on experience, one on an anecdote from a friend and one on a newspaper report of a rugby player I had once played against, killed by an accident of falling wood while at work on a construction site in the docks.

Three have since been published, two still waiting. "Mr Roopratna's Chocolate" won the Rhys Davies Short Story Prize and a thousand pound cheque in 1999. "Feeding the House Crows" was published in two anthologies, *Mama's Baby (Papa's Maybe)* and *From the Ashes,* earning £30 and a Newport United Football kit respectively. (Although I've never received the football kit) "This Time of Year" was translated and published in the Croation new fiction book *Kolo*, earning a trip to Zagreb courtesy of the British Council. It was also published in *Cambrensis* short story magazine, for which I was paid the standard three free copies. I have not submitted "Tom's Castle" or "When the Woman Sings" to any magazine as yet. This is a question of time and energy. "Mr Roopratna's Chocolate" has been lucrative. It has earned a clear £700 more than any other story I have written. But I have hesitated in sending any more out. They do not earn enough money to make it worthwhile. I will wait now for enough work to carry a collection.

In *For Love and Money*, Jonathan Raban talks about setting himself up a number of fronts to capitalise as a writer, to become Hugo Williams's classic urban scrounger. But Raban warns against the risks of this.

"Malcolm Bradbury and I had talked of the difficulty of freelancing for a living and he'd used the word diversification. It was like working in any other industry, he said; you had to learn to diversify, cutting and running from fiction to journalism, broadcasting to print. I took him up more literally than I think he intended, and tried to set myself up on so many fronts that I deserved to fail on every one of them."

I know what he means. Since 1993, with various degrees of success and failure I have written and been paid for novels, short stories, stage plays, radio documentaries, screenplay treatments, screenplay scripts, soap opera scripts, travel articles, speculative essays and book reviews. Indirectly I have taught creative writing workshops in schools, universities and writers' centres. I have lectured on writing and publishing, appeared on tv posing as a script writer, author and publisher, while on radio as a reviewer and commentator. I have also helped to set up and run a publishing company.

This does not include the work that has occupied my time and is in no way connected with writing. Building, care work, painting and house management have all provided temporary gainful employment. These interludes can be useful. Work recreates itself as fiction.

As a freelance writer it is unwise to turn work down. Money is fickle and small scale work often leads to more. Money also tends to be irregular and ephemeral although there can be the occasional lucky break. I once received two cheques from the BBC for a very similar piece of work. The only reason I had the commission in the first place was because I had asked Karl Francis an awkward question in a discussion on television drama in the Cardiff Literary Festival. It was along the lines of "If BBC Wales continues to ignore Welsh viewers, will they continue to ignore BBC Wales?" At the time Karl Francis was a freelance director but within a month he had been appointed Head of Drama at the BBC in Cardiff. A phone call and a speculative commission followed.

It has been a good few years. I have managed to live and not be consciously short of money. I have not made a fortune, but except for mortgages I have no debts. The threat of unemployment lurks in the background, but as a writer there is always hope. It costs very little to sit down and write. The problems lie in the commitments that surround and contain you. Family, children, the food bill. At present I can still afford time away from Cardiff. My wife and children walk in as I write this. We are renting a cottage in Cornwall for a week. It is half term. They have left me in peace for the morning but have now returned for lunch. I am trying to finish this essay.

For Cyril Connolly in *Enemies of Promise*, one of the greatest dangers for a writer was the pram in the hallway.

Jonathan Raban has a lot of time for Connolly and his literary hero, Shelleyblake, the young, under-employed writer.

In *Enemies of Promise* one of the aims of the under-employed writer is to review books. It seems like a good scam, getting paid to read and then offer your opinions, in print, for people to read. I first offered my services to the national newspaper back in 1991. *"It was a rejection but good practice."* But in 1998 I met the literary editor of *The Western Mail*, Mario Basini. It was a Sunday morning and he was writing a story on the closure of Chapter and Verse, a Cardiff bookshop. I was in the bookshop packing it away, helping it close. I asked him did he have any books I could perhaps review? This turned into a fairly regular slot reviewing books for *The Western Mail*.

"Shadily living by one's literary wits is as good a way of making too little money as any other, "

Dylan Thomas replying to the *Horizon* questionaire.

Over a two year period I reviewed 48 books. It paid twenty-five pounds per review, but I got to read a lot of unusual work and also got to keep or sell on the books. It provided a useful supplementary income and I was writing. About half were actually printed. Mario has now given up the literary editor's post and the books have stopped appearing in the mail. Fortunately just now I have more work than I need. Scripts for the HTV drama *Nuts and Bolts* more than compensate for a lack of reviewing. But series do not last for ever and I will need to diversify again. I know a radio producer who is now heading the BBC Wales radio drama *Station Road*. I have never written drama for radio.

Another year on and *Station Road* has been cut by the BBC. *Nuts and Bolts* has reformed its writing team. I am not in it. I have a letter from Alison Hindell, a radio producer for BBC Wales asking for ideas. I have a meeting with a theatre director to discuss a new play. There are no promises.

"Mr Roopratna's Chocolate" was turned down for radio

transmission on the grounds that the meaning of the story was not clear enough for radio listeners. In the end you can choose to write for the market or ignore it.

My stories are built on experience or the telling of another story to change it into something else. It is unfortunate if a story is taken just from the life and then simply termed a fiction. Life produces many stories but the fictional lens gives us the depth of experience or just the enjoyment that a simple story from the world of ordinary lives will not produce. The world of the ordinary is fascinating beyond the simple expediencies of life. The great true stories are just as they purport to be. Great writing is about unique experience turned into the universality of fiction.

"The only writing that was any good was what you made up, what you imagined." Ernest Hemingway in conversation with George Plimpton, *Paris Review*

But in this Hemingway is only telling a half truth. "Big Two Hearted River" is based on his experiences of fishing a trout river in his youth. The background to the story is a soldier returning from the first world war and coming to terms with the way the world has changed. He has changed and the world has broken him but he senses if he keeps going the world will change again. Hemingway has used his knowledge of fishing and his direct experience of the Italian front in World War I to create the story as fiction. In this form, fiction is inevitably imagination and experience working together.

My Piece of Happiness is drawn from my experience as a Day Service Officer for the then South Glamorgan Social Services. I was involved with a team setting up service plans for individuals with severe learning difficulties. This in turn involved contact with professionals providing other aspects of service provision, such as the accommodation and resettlement of individuals moving out of Ely residential hospital into community housing. Our job at the Small Scale

Day Service was to provide individual, tailored day activity plans for people at the furthest end of the learning difficulty range. Very few of the people I worked with had speech ability and most were unable to walk or attend to basic physical needs. The team was based in an old Edwardian house on Richmond Road but with a service that was designed to be community based, revolving around the needs of the people we were employed to work with. They lived either at home with their families or at Ely Hospital awaiting resettlement into the community. I only needed to be in the office about one day a week. Less when I could manage it. It was a good job which I enjoyed. It introduced me to many people I would never otherwise have met, including my wife and a part of society I had had little contact with previously. As a writer whose work is very much based in the fictional present, it was a subject that was going to find its way into my work and fiction. But the various versions of *My Piece of Happiness*, although derived from the world I worked within, are not mirror reflections of it.

To convert experience through the fictional prism is the ultimate luxury and responsibility of the writer. Nothing is exactly as you remember it, everything is open to interpretation. Most of the characters in *My Piece of Happiness* have echoes of personalities. But they are not just those people; they are someone apart.

"I've written a number of stories about the Michigan country – the country is always true – what happens in the stories is fiction."
    Ernest Hemingway in a letter to his father. Paris, 20th March, 1925.

Within the character George, for instance, there is the figure of Peter Grant, the subject of the book's dedication. He is a strange, fascinating, committed man. George in the book is from Cardiff via London and the Army, likes jazz, used to box. Pete Grant was in the army but has no interest in jazz and used to play football. I have no idea where he is from but would guess it's a city. He is happily married, used to drink too much and has delusions of persecution. George is unhappily single, drinks too much and lives in a one bedroom flat in Riverside. They have both spent time in psychiatric institutions and both have attempted to burn down the headquarters of Cardiff Social Services. In the book, George is left at the end, contemplating another solitary winter after being rejected by Angel. There is a suggestion that there are more serious consequences for him, but they are only suggestions. Pete served 12 months of a two year sentence for arson.

The man I know as George is not Pete Grant although he shares some of his history. If I think of anyone as George I will see Dorien Thomas but he is fading now, and perhaps when we film the screenplay he will have another face and another colour. I see George as someone else and perhaps also as me, an alter ego I don't want to become because I know him too well. Although I have no real understanding of Pete Grant beyond friendship, I do have a knowledge of myself and this is perhaps an examination of the self in the minds of others.

In *The Unbearable Lightness of Being*, Milan Kundera suggests that fiction is an investigation of life in the trap the world has become. This is given full force in the title's resonance, which echoes throughout the book. But fiction is only a trap if your world is closed. I like to believe the world is open. The fiction then becomes a portrayal of the truths of reality, but also of enjoyment and celebration. In "Big Two Hearted River", Nick Adams is celebrating the fact that he is still alive in the beauty of a fishing trip up country. Much of the land has been burned over by strip felling, but he knows they can't have burned over all the land and that if he walks far enough, he will reach clean unfelled forest and find a good camp for the night. Nothing is said of his past but it is there, like the grasshoppers that skip ahead of him. They have turned black to match the ash. He knows they have changed but he knows they will change back as the forest greens.

My Piece of Happiness attempts to be a celebration of change. George has to change to engage with his own life, and Sean must reach his own decisions so that he can have his own piece of happiness. But they were all real people that have waited with me to become fiction. What is left out for George is his fate.

Sunday evening used to be chapel with Andy. They both enjoyed the singing. There was not much point in going alone. He didn't find he had so much to do lately, Sunday or the week. Still he needed to be clean.

My Piece of Happiness

The fiction leaves room for readers to engage their own imagination, interpretation. I believe George has got away with the fire at the office. He has lost his job but he didn't get caught for anything else. But he could be on bail, waiting for the court case that will bury him for years. Arson is a serious offence.

I want the reader to decide.

The process of these worlds becoming fictional is a transitional process that has taken the eight years since I resigned from the department. The friendships I made have lasted longer than the job, as has my enduring interest in the subject. The world now of actual memory has become the world of my fictional memory. It is a process that is still continuing even as I move away from the writing.

The Play

The last months of 1997 are filled with the discussion of practicalities. The designer arrives with a design for the set. We will force the easy realism of the play against a sharp minimalist set of grey and white lighted walls. I love the idea. It is a set for a real play. A real play that will open in the late days of January, 1998 for a ten day run. There will be a three week rehearsal period. There is talk of moving the play onto other venues, The Donmar Warehouse in London is interested in a Welsh play but not in us. Jeff and Rebecca Gould, the assistant director, go on a tour of old miners' welfare halls in the valleys, but nothing ever comes of rumours.

I have nothing more to write now but letters and a host of invites exhorting people to come.

Talking About Football - a rehearsal

"This is the morning I get bored and talk about football, then argue about what line where."
Jeff Teare, Artistic Director, Made In Wales

Two weeks in and I'm sitting in rehearsals waiting for the actors to try a run without a script. James and Dorien are talking about papers on a park bench in the rehearsal room.

They try the first run and Jeff stops them five minutes in. They are still struggling to get the words in order. He offers them some consolation. "A difficult script to remember, fiendishly difficult."

The ten days to here are filled with discussion on the script. Actors with opinions, honing the words and asking about ideas. New words: through lines, beats and super-objective. All have meaning, shining briefly.

I find my way slowly through this world.

The days are the words. Evenings are the pubs close to the theatre. Dorien is ensconced in The Butchers' back room, lunch-time and evening. He's developing a series of board games based on Navajo and Hopi traditions. He enlists James and me to play in the corner of the room. I don't like The Butchers' much. I feel as if I'm in the back-room of an old uncle I don't like anymore.

The Insole is more open, and when we can persuade Dorien we end up there.

The mornings are dark. I'm catching a bus at twenty to

eight. This is the first time I've ever caught a bus to work for five days in a row. It's the first time I've ever caught a bus to work. By the time the day is over I catch the bus back in darkness. Gill waits uneasily with Tai. The theatre is a new world where I am away from her.

I should have written this as we ploughed through but I was too absorbed with the feeling of the week in which the days were bleak and light at the same time.

The second break and Jeff discusses a beat on the death of Sean's mother. I listen to all this now. Last week I spoke and thought loads. The attention to lines and their individual meanings amazes me. You can't throw away a line, there must be a reason, a through line for everything.

The first few days I talk and discuss everything with Gill. She soon gets tired of this.

Eleven, Tuesday morning. Lowri and Sharon arrive. The second scene. We talk in the break about reviewers, Mike Leigh, who Jeff has worked with, and the lack of a national paper in Wales.

A scream from Lowri runs through the room and me. The week before I enjoyed watching these people work. Sharon doesn't come out to drink after the day's work; she has a young daughter at home. Lowri is out on other nights. A strange mix of ideas and energy. She plays with the world.

The week is full of stories. Jeff and his stories of work at the National. Dorien, life in Pontypridd. Sharon, charming and reserved, speaks rarely, finding the words easier in silence.

Thursday, second week. Daniel Morden is waiting at the bottom of the stairs. We have a couple of drinks at The Butchers'. James, Lowri and Dorien play games at the next table.

Friday. I remember now the nights and a few moments of the discussions. I enjoy the re-writing when it works. Other times I pull away.

Tuesday. The long office scene. Everyone on, bar James. It stretches into five false starts in a row. David finally gets a line. Jeff speaking, more beats and suggestions. My ideas are last week now. This is the script we will work with.

Long talk over a line. "Unless you want to ask him yourself?" Dorien suggests it is dramatic gibberish. I decide not to change. Another disagreement on the script with Dorien. Unease, as Jeff doesn't like the line either. However I do, so he'll have to do it this time. It takes them another week and another argument to get me to realise the line is dead.

My mind turns through this week as I imagine an afternoon in the sun.

The actors try a new emphasis and the scene shifts. George is now heading down. Dorien is trying to get more darkness out of the character and the play. I am resisting. The world I am writing about has enough shades for me now.

The sun is out this afternoon. Clear blue skies over the city, air from the north. I sit in the rehearsal room.

Thursday afternoon. Gill's birthday: the 22nd of January. A stagger through the second half of the play. The words are difficult, not sticking. "A multiplicity of meaning or totally devoid of content" as Dorien suggested in the bar of The Insole. Lowri's words fly around the stage now. James moves closer. She plays the little girl smiling.

I think where this play is taking me.

Test and George argue it all. One of the better scenes in the play.

I miss a couple of scenes and there's a change in tone from Sean that I hate.

We shall see what the discussion brings.

Full cast on Friday morning. First full run through. The video refuses to work. The actors move around, preparing themselves. Not sure what that means. They talk a lot. And now it starts.

The afternoon, rehearsal and notes. Becky and Jan tell me to sit it out. I'm not needed. I decide I am, so sit here anyway.

Monday. We plan the week, trying to fit an audience into the various nights. Wednesday is a sell-out but the other nights are patchy.

I talk to Sharon in the break about Welsh theatre. Theatr Clwyd is in the news this morning over a suspect lottery grant. She is passionate and eloquent about a subject she loves.

The rehearsals pickup speed. The actors working hard across the play. They begin to gel as people begin to enjoy working together.

The darkness lifts again this morning after a difficult weekend. A storm has swept across the city, disturbing slates and fences and worrying our neighbour's gate into pieces. Gill is away in the Midlands. I resist running around Blackweir and knock a gate back together instead.

Jeff gives a few well thought out notes. I begin to love this life again.

Tuesday, the pace quickens as we tech the show. The actors firing on the tensions of the theatre and the prospect of a live audience tonight.

I'm sitting in the bar again listening to the words fill the space. I need to take a few more photographs.

Wednesday afternoon. Twelve hours after last night. The public dress, filled with a few actors and friends. Pete Grant only staying for half of the show but very enthusiastic afterwards. Lowri asks him, "Did you burn a building down?" Dorien and David stand on the front of the stage, messing around with some music hall number I've never heard of. The production team run a re-tech for tonight's opening. A full house of friends and friends of the company.

I'm not sure what I feel about this now.

The words of the tech fill the room in a shorthand I don't understand.

Last few minutes before the people start to arrive. The show is fine, perhaps too short for a full run now but it's there.

For a new draft I'd put in a scene with Grigeli and George. Last regrets.

I sit near the back with Gill, the play rises to a full house.

Moving On

It is a diary of sorts. An attempt to invoke some of the flow of the three weeks in rehearsal that seem both fractured and solid. The pieces fit together now as they must have during the process. But it was a tunnel, absorbed within the rehearsal for three dark weeks in January before the light of the show surrounded us. I cannot write of it as anything less than a collaboration. I did not feel exposed as the writer but absorbed within the weight of the company. I feel my writing improved. I learned about the theatre, process and form. I felt lucky. I enjoyed it all.

At the end of a run the family again disperses. There could be a feeling of loss but I don't feel it. I think the production has gone as well as it possibly could have. A sell out final few nights, some good reviews and people laughing and obviously enjoying themselves. The play has been a success.

And I have another performance to roll into. Jeff is staging a three part production to commemorate the first world war and I get a commission for thirty minutes about a soldier who has escaped from the war only to be betrayed by his friends. It is a true story told to me by a priest who used to minister at a church in Port Talbot. I enjoy the research, write thirty pages while on a trip to Spain and the production swings into three weeks with students from the Welsh College of Music and Drama at the Museum of Welsh Life. Spring starts late and *Little Country, Big War* struggles for a few nights before the audience gets going. Then the theatre world closes away again. I know I must move back to prose fiction.

My Piece of Happiness is still in my mind. I re-read the

script and immediately write another three scenes, one of which should have been in the play and perhaps if another performance was tried, all of them. In the longer version George and Sean's sister have a scene which is perhaps the beginning of an affair. George's relationship with Angel is forced to the point where she rejects him and finally a longer development of Angel and George's confrontation in the office over Sean's future home. But they are now sketches for the novel I want to finish. I reckon I have three months before I run out of money. It is always a balance of time against money. I need to write when there is enough money not to worry immediately about any more.

Within the pages of Waterstone's *The Cost of Letters* there is a recommendation that writers should rent out rooms in their house as a means of securing an income. I understood from the first few years of trying to sell words that writing would only produce a fickle return. In some instances I have been fortunate. But I made a conscious attempt to diversify my sources of income so that I would be able to support my writing through other means. I come from a background of hard manual work. I have run a demolition business and worked as a fishermen on the Australian coast. Manual work can bring its own rewards, one of which is a certain independence. The pay is not good but there is always another job.

    During the last ten years I have been able to supplement any income I have been able to earn as a writer by labouring work for my father on a variety of building sites from Seven Sisters to Skewen. I had to commute forty miles each way to every site and sometimes worked away for the week. But I was earning money, paid at the end of the week, and I was working for my father. This additional source of income was crucial to any stability I have been able to maintain as a writer and also lately as a publisher. As a bricklayer I was also able to raise a mortgage to buy the house I had first lived in when I came to

Cardiff. I would not have been able to do this as a writer.

When my father read an early draft of this work he commented that I had never been a bricklayer. This is true. But reading the passage again I have only claimed that as a bricklayer I was able to raise a mortgage, which is again true. This is fiction depending on how the words are interpreted. For the bank lending me money it was important that I was a bricklayer; for my father it is important that I was not.

I start to write again at 53, Colum Road. I have a room in the house to live in as an office away from home. A new baby brings a lot of additions with it. *The Enemies of Promise* warns against prams in the hallway. 53 Colum Road has a hallway filled with bicycles. There are other rooms, rented, which help to pay the mortgage of an itinerant builder/writer.

Playing with the Novel

I begin re-writing the novel. The voices call easily from my head. The script is a significant extension of the short novel I had first finished during the early summer of 1995.

At this stage it is important to develop a routine again. Again I work in the mornings, perhaps four mornings a week. The house is quiet and the room is the one I lived in when I first came to Cardiff in 1989 to begin writing.

I write without a break for three hours which is usually the extent of a writing day. It is easier to work from the bones of the play as a framework, but the space that prose affords allows for more digressions, diversions in the text. Despite this I am careful to keep to the tight framework that the play has created. I am aiming for a story well told, and I am contemptuous of the literary tricks that fill many modern novels with air. The book will have a simple two act structure that the play would have finally attained. The only experiments are the short chapters concentrating on Sean sitting in a chair watching the tv. They aim to represent an increase in understanding or consciousness that Sean experiences throughout the book. The words, as they describe this progressive but-essentially-the-same scene, become more complicated, descriptive, representative of Sean's growing extension into life as he essentially gets pieces of his happiness and life together. Each scene is named after figures from within the religions of Japan, primarily Shintoism but also extending into Japanese Zen. Hotei, Ebisu, Fukorokuju, Jurojin, Daikoku, Benten, Bishamon which all represent different aspects of contentment, good fortune or happiness. These figures appear throughout Japanese storytelling and are also figuratively represented within the artistic tradition. The book when finally published contained commissioned drawings by the artist Maldwyn Griffiths of the gods named in the scenes representing the development of Sean's awareness.

I do not think the representations of these gods of good fortune affected the creative process of writing but the theme of the pursuit of happiness in its various guises is central to the book.

The book in another draft is completed by June. I submit it to the Arts Council through Parthian for a production grant and to Norman Schwenk for a final opinion. It has a new opening. The final paper shop scene in the play is now mirrored by one at the start of the book as George enters and negotiates a job for Sean. This is a result of a suggestion by a reader who assessed the play for publication. I liked the idea and wrote the chapter immediately. The story in play form will be published in September 1998. But the new submission is for a novel. The story must hold as a novel and not be just a converted drama text. Norman Schwenk is quick to read the manuscript he is now very familiar with, having read or seen at least three different versions. He suggests I have taken the book as far as I can. It is as finished as it can be. The Arts Council of Wales reader's report criticises the book as being too representative of a television play and particularly dislikes the realism of the narrative. A grant is refused. I ignore the advice and re-submit the book unchanged for a second opinion on the next round of applications. The book this time with a different reader is approved. A strong recommendation in favour is offered and congratulations to the writer on the efforts made since the reader has first read the manuscript.

All books produce different opinions, but I have confidence in the readability of this novel. My only concerns are the subject matter. I am not sure that the central story of George flanked by Sean and Sarah will interest enough people to make them want to read it. The mainstream of commercially successful literature at present lies somewhere between novels that are about their readers and novels that are about lives that readers find either exotic or enviable. A third category may be termed escapist. *My Piece of Happiness* does not fall easily into any of these categories. Obviously there are exceptions. And good writing should always find a market. It depends on your market.

My Piece of Happiness portrays lives that are not to be envied. It is realist and offers little escapism. I believe it is about a common pursuit of happiness, but people do not necessarily want to read how difficult this can be. James Kelman is one writer who has been successful, artistically and commercially in writing about this territory. *A Diasaffection* is about the nervous breakdown of a teacher trying to find a sense to his life, and is a book which pulled me into mournful self reflection. I had to abandon it with forty pages to go in case I had my own nervous breakdown. *Not, Not While the Giro*, by the same author, a realist selection of working class stories, is more bearable. These are stories and novels Kelman needed to write. In his acceptance speech on winning the Booker prize in 1995 he railed against the metropolitan establishment for trying to dictate the terms of his engagement with fiction.

"My culture and my language have the right to exist and no one has the authority to dismiss that right."

For me *My Piece of Happiness* is a story I wanted to tell. The art is in the way the story is exposed. The reviews are more sympathetic to the book than I considered likely. But the reviews are by readers commenting on the art of fiction.

These concerns are perhaps confirmed with the failure of the manuscript to make any impact with London publishers. The English department of Cardiff University has periodic contacts with London agents and Norman Schwenk gave my name to David Riding of the MBA literary agency who have an office off the Tottenham Court Road. I had made several attempts to find an agent to represent my work before the publication of *Tree of Crows* and *Freeways*. The latter produced some interest but no firm offers. I gave up on the idea of finding an agent, coming to the conclusion that they eventually find writers. In this way David Riding sent me a preliminary letter of enquiry which prompted a CV, *Freeways* and *Happiness* in response. He invited me to London and a contract of representation was in the post the following day. It was a tremendous boost to the ego to be finally represented by a London literary agent. As a writer you are a free man in the sense that you make your own choices, but in a world of industrial publication and marketing-led decisions the writer is isolated. An agency brings to a writer defence, negotiation of contracts and opportunities within a wider world of literature. Although David Riding was going to try to secure a publication deal for *My Piece of Happiness* I was realistic about its chances with a London publisher for a largely unknown writer with an unlikely and uncommercial product.

And so it proved. David Riding began representing my work in the spring of 1999. *My Piece of Happiness* was in theory ready to publish during the Summer of 1999, but I decided to hold publication with Parthian for a year to see if any offers from London were forthcoming. There weren't any.

The Final Play

At this stage of my writing career I was fortunate to be the publishing editor/managing director/salesman/bookpacker for Parthian Books. The resolve to publish *My Piece of Happiness* found expression in the original switch of the work from a stage play into a short novel. The publishing company was still a small concern but flexible.

During a year of dormancy I altered the manuscript by a few words. There was some final editing, and a number of the switches in tense were evened out. The rest was waiting. The reading and commenting on this book was over until the reviews. There is a limit to the amount of constructive criticism you can allow into your work as a writer before you lose the individuality of voice. *My Piece of Happiness* was already a collaborative work. I felt I could not afford to allow other voices of influence into the book.

I write this in February 2001, ten months after the publication of the book. It has sold 354 copies and received seven reviews. I feel the time of the book has yet to come. I keep getting odd encouraging letters from people who have read it. People who have usually had some experience with the subject; people in the end, for whom the book was written. Sometimes I feel I can't get away from the subject. I want to return to it. But things have changed and the world, my world, moves on. Made in Wales has had its Arts Council grant cut completely and now exists as a company only in name. Pete Grant is long released from prison. He continues with a novel that he is writing while providing a challenge for the staff at the job centre. He rings me occasionally and we meet for breakfast. I think he appreciated the words at the front of the book. James Westaway, the actor who played Sean in the stage version died of a brain haemorrhage in April 2000. I will always see him as Sean, but I miss him as a friend. The book holds a dedication to him, but it is only words.

What It Means

I re-read this essay, the reviews, then the book again. The time has gone. I cannot separate it from my life. In reflection it is no easier. The novel is a process of attrition. You get an idea and work through it to its conclusion. Many more novels are started than are finished. Attrition, perseverance, time, luck all have varying parts to play.

In the book *Welsh Journal* by Jeremy Hooker, an account of ten years teaching and writing in Wales, there is a long articulated cry for the writer on the margins. Hooker lays bare his own insecurities and fear for himself as a writer failing to recognise his voice and find an audience. He is aware of Baldwin's world of indifference but unable to inure himself against it. There is a despair running through Hooker's journals that I recognise but don't share. Everything seems to be subservient to his writing. Stephen King in his instructional book *On Writing* is a writer always in favour of what he calls fine times. They may not produce any work, but they are in the end fine times. For Hooker the poetry seems to mean everything and he is acutely aware that his position remains unrecognised and misunderstood. His work is marginalised by lack of recognition and also by his position as an exile in Wales surrounded by a language he doesn't understand and a culture he can't embrace. From this he produces some fine work. But his life beyond poetry doesn't seem to hold much joy for him. His wife is hardly mentioned or has been edited out. His son and daughter only appear for artistic and poetic resonance. But still he writes, producing a troubling and troubled memoir. The need to create silences everything else. I do not have this.

I consider I have written a fair amount of work in ten years of writing, but when I look back the periods of actual writing were limited. The rest was living, some fine times, some bleak; most, just living.

I still feel the pleasure in writing but there are other

pursuits. I recently had a conversation with the critic John Pikoulis. We were waiting for a poetry reading to begin at Chapter Arts Centre. Pikoulis had been very complimentary about my first novel, *WSR*, but recently his opinions have cooled. I suspect this is because I have failed to fit into his model of a Welsh working class writer, but this may be my own prejudice. Perhaps he just doesn't like the books? He asked about my doctoral thesis, but not about my writing. I told him I was working on a new book. Not a lie but a half-truth. He claimed that I was not a writer anymore but a businessman. The poet at the reading was published by Parthian.

Sometimes I think he is correct. But then this may have been a necessity of the times. Without the company, the rented houses and the resolve to keep sending out the work, most of my writing would not have appeared.

In the autumn of 2001 the novel is re-issued as a paperback, a lower price, a new cover, the same words except for one. I removed the word "fat" from page seven. In launching the novel the author is often exposed to the trial of public reading. I can't complain to the publisher because I am the publisher, but I am also the writer and I want the words to be read, the story understood. During the readings I always remove the word "fat" from the description of a woman on Cowbridge Road. I realise in my mind that she is not "fat" but weighed and rounded by old age. I also do not like saying someone is fat. I do not have the resolve to read the rest of the book for further editing. I have given as much energy as I can to the project. This essay stretches my commitment further. It is a dissection of the creative process through my writing of the book and through the prism of selected other works which have influenced me both directly and indirectly. Some of these writers have written specifically on the creation of work, others more obliquely through letters and even through the fictional text itself. Moving one's self away from the process to dissect that process gives perspective but also a fear of the unknown. I know how I created the work in terms of commitment, hours spent, re-wording, collaboration, but it is not a template. I could not do it again. But, again from Hemingway, to quote from an interview with George Plimpton in the *Paris Review*.

"From things that have happened and from things as they exist and from all things that you know and all those you cannot know, you make something through your invention that is not a representation but a whole new thing truer than anything true and alive, and you make it alive, and if you make it well enough, you give it immortality."

I finish this to complete my thoughts on the words and the process of the novel. Five years of consideration and eight years of work soaking into the time of yesterday. I feel I need to leave the book go. Allow it to find its own time.

Aberteifi, July 2003

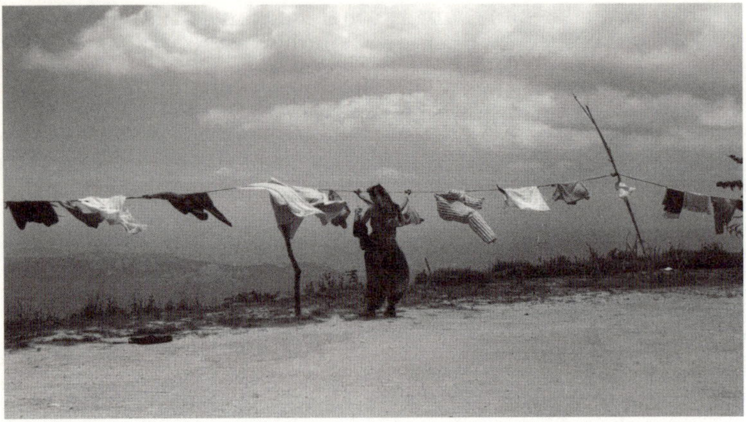

The rest was living, some fine times, some bleak; most, just living.

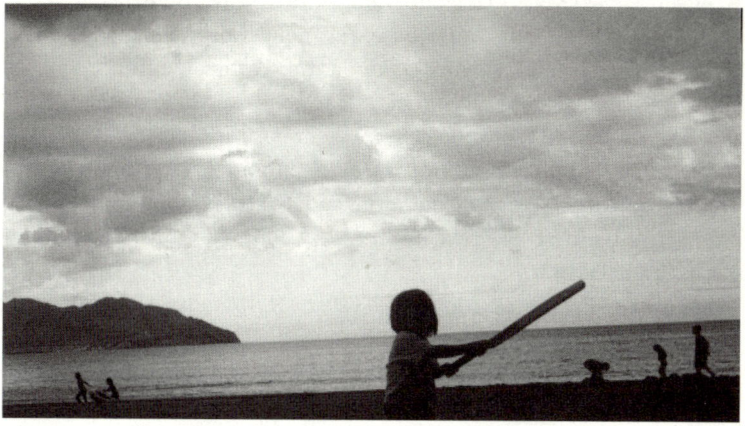

Some sources

Baker, Carlos. *Ernest Hemingway, A Life Story*. London: Collins, 1969.
Baldwin, James. *Notes of a Native Son*. Harmondsworth: Penguin, 1995.
Connolly, Cyril. *Enemies of Promise*. Harmondsworth: Penguin, 1961.
Evans, George Brinley. *Boys of Gold*. Cardiff: Parthian, 2000.
Graves, Robert. *Goodbye to All That*. Harmondsworth: Penguin, 1972.
Holgate, Andrew & Wilson-Fletcher, Honor ed. *The Cost of Letters: A Survey of Literary Living Standards*. Brentford: Waterstone's, 1998.
Hooker, Jeremy. *Welsh Journal*. Bridgend: Seren, 2001.
Hemingway, Ernest. *Selected Letters, 1917-1961*, ed Carlos Baker. New York: Granada, 1981.
Hemingway, Ernest. *A Moveable Feast*. Harmondsworth: Penguin, 1973.
Hemingway, Ernest. *The Essential Ernest Hemingway*. (Includes *In Our Time*. New York: 1925 & "Winner Take Nothing". New York: 1933) Harmondsworth: Penguin, 1964.
Kelman, James. *Not, Not While the Giro*. London: Pan, 1993.
Kelman, James. *A Disaffection*. London: Pan, 1995.
King, Stephen. *On Writing*. London: Hodder & Stoughton, 2001.
Kundera, Milan. *The Unbearable Lightness of Being*. London: Faber & Faber, 1984.
Lynn, Kenneth.S. *Hemingway*. Cambridge: Harvard, 1995.
Meyers, Jeffrey. *Hemingway, A Biography*. London: Macmillan, 1988.
Plimpton, George. Ernest Hemingway in Conversation, in George Plimpton ed. *Writers at Work*, London: Martin Secker & Warburg, 1963.
Raban, Jonathan. *For Love and Money*. Macmillan: London, 1988.
Steinbeck, John. *The Grapes of Wrath*. London: Pan, 1975.
Steinbeck, John. *Of Mice and Men*. London: Pan, 1980.
Steinbeck, John. *The Moon is Down*. London: Pan, 1971.
Steinbeck, John. *A Life in Letters*. Edited by Elaine Steinbeck & Robert Wallsten. London: Minerva, 1994.

Jo Menell and The John Morgan Award

The John Morgan Award was set up through the efforts of Jo Menell to commemorate his friend and associate John Morgan who died in 1988.

The Award was supported by a distinguished group of patrons and a dedicated board of trustees who administered an annual travel writing award for Welsh writers.

It has had a significant impact on the development of Welsh writing in the wider world context. It has supported speculative projects resulting in books by Robert Minhinnick – *Watching the Fire Eater;* Nigel Jenkins – *Gwalia in Khasia*; Jon Gower – *An Island Called Smith* and my own book *Freeways* which developed out of an essay on migrant workers in California.

I would like to express my personal thanks to Jo Menell for the support of the award over a decade of development and to John Morgan for providing the inspiration.

Lewis Davies